GUNS

OF

CAIN

Also by J. Spencer Bryant

The Chef

Also by Max Bain

Loser's Serendipity

Heads or Tails

GUNS
OF
CAIN

THE ULTIMATE WESTERN NOVEL

J. SPENCER BRYANT
MAX BAIN

Alliance Books
an imprint of
Harlan Publishing Company
Summerfield, North Carolina USA

HARLAN
PUBLISHING

Guns of Cain is a work of fiction. Any references to real people, events, establishments, organizations, or locales are intended only to give the fiction a sense of reality and authenticity. Other names, characters, places, and incident portrayed herein are either the product of the author's imagination or are used fictionally. The views expressed in this book are purely those of the characters

Published by Alliance Books
P.O. Box 397
Summefield, North Carolina 27358

Book and Cover Design by Jeff Pate

First Edition

ISBN: 0-9747278-4-9

Library of Congress Control Number: 2004

Acknowledgements

I wish to thank Leon and Brenda Buynum, Mattie Sellers, James Foxx, Jimmy Whitley, and others who helped in many ways to bring this story to publication. And to Max Bain who saw the worth of the story to lend his valuable talent.

From the Author

As an Afro-American man, I have and had often thought about black men and their relationship to situations during the old west. Perhaps others have also; however, I chose to write a story of a poignant situation that no doubt happened, but was never written about or told.

I have been a western fan for a long time, and had found evidence in writings and pictures of black men in the west, but never anything of importance in their deeds or actions. Yet we know they were there and played a role in the development of the old west.

This western novel was written mostly in 1940 and stayed around all this time due to the times that had to change in order for the story of a black man and their relationships with whites in the old west to be accepted.

At this time and now that I'm 83 years of age, this story is being told with the help of fellow author Max Bain.

This book is dedicated to my mother who, in spite of everything, still believed in me. JSB

This one's for Jules...MB

ONE

The clock behind the desk in the Phillips Hotel chimed three times. The hotel clerk, wearing a shade over his eyes, stirred from his catnap. Looking at the clock in disgust, he emptied his wad of chewing tobacco with a thud into the spittoon. Without getting up, the clerk stretched and grunted before settling into the old stuffed horse-chair to finish his nap.

Outside the hotel, the withered frame building cast ominous shadows along the main dirt street leading in and out of town. Although a bright moon shone, the many lights beamed from the Dipper Saloon on one side of the street and from the Payday Casino on the other side. The bank, the general store and other small shops separated both places of gaiety and their lights bade welcome, even outshining that of the moon.

At three o'clock in the morning such a light would be strange in any other town, but here in Pueblo, located in the southeastern part of Colorado, it was the usual sight. The town itself boasted of growth through the many different people and trades. Yet to the lone man walking in the middle of the street, it made no difference, at least not now. But he knew in a town as large and still growing like Pueblo was, anything could happen or be expected.

A gentle breeze tugged at the stranger's shoestring tie and flipped his coattail to and fro. Mindful of the breeze and its freshness on this warm June morning, the tall stranger made his way past one building and then another until he reached the Phillips Hotel. It seemed as if hours had passed since old Hap Russell, the night clerk, had awakened. This time it was due to the tapping of the bell on the desk. Hap blinked and rose slowly from the chair, scratching his chin as he took in the full view of this stranger. The cut of the stranger's eastern broadcloth suit made the old man's eyes widen, especially the bright yellow, brocaded vest, with a heavy watch chain draped across it into the small pocket. Hap was also careful to notice the man wore no guns. This sort of made him breathe easier.

Hap spoke, "I hanker you want a room, eh?"

"Yeah," smiled the stranger, "for about a couple of months, with food."

Hap nodded, "That'll be..."

But before Hap could finish his sentence, the stranger tossed a twenty dollar gold piece on the counter telling him to keep the change.

"Just put your marker onto the book," said Hap, watching the stranger's bold hand write the neat lettering."

"You from the east, eh, Mr. Clinton?" Hap inquired after looking at the entry.

"That's right, in part."

"Well," said Hap, "folks 'round here call me Hap. I don't own the hotel, but you'll no doubt see Mr. Phillips around. He's the owner. You ain't got no baggage?" he added.

"No," answered Clay Clinton, "but I'll pick up plenty before I leave."

Clay Clinton, tall and lean with a leather tan face, turned and walked up the steps leading to his room. It was then Hap noticed the medium-sized package wrapped in chamois.

"Humph," he snorted, "that's a queer one."

Before Clay went to bed, he unwrapped the package he carried, carefully inspecting the two ivory-handled Colts. They were beautiful, with a secret undertone of a violent thing. The worn butts bespoke use, but anyone could see their condition was fine. Clay also unwrapped another smaller package, and from this he took a brown-papered cigarette, lit it, and walked to the window. Raising it, he looked out through the haze of smoke from his ready-rolled cigarette. He could see the Payday and the Dipper. The bank with its adobe and frame structure sat beside the general store, and across the street beyond the hitching rails sat the women's shop as well as the harness and leather shop.

He smiled as his mind raced back to his reason for coming to Pueblo in the first place. With a grimace his smile turned to a set, curious, cold laugh. He could hear Major Campton saying,

"Damn you, Clay, you're only thirty-two years old, and I'm appointing you to U.S. Marshal whether you like it or not. The fact that you're my nephew has nothing to do with it, there's simply not another man who can handle the job. Now get your ass on into Pueblo, clean up that hellhole and then you can turn in your badge. I know you spent the years with the Rangers and now you want to kick up your heels," he added, "but do this job and trust me to take care of the rest."

"Hell, sir," explained Clay, "I just don't want this part of the country; I'd rather work in California. But I'll take the job, on one condition."

"Well, what is it, man? You name it and I'll take care of it."

"Just this," Clay answered, "I work this job my own way – not undercover and with no orders from anyone else but you. I only want to deal with one man. And," he added. "If I need anything, or any information, I want it sent right away."

After considering Clay's requests for a few minutes, his uncle agreed.

"All right," he said, "I'll see to that. And here's one month's pay in advance." Then he asked, "You know what to look for, right. Or didn't Hargrave tell you?"

"All I know is that the government thinks there's a gang operating out of Pueblo into four surrounding states, getting nothing but government gold and currency, with a few killings thrown in."

"That about covers it," his uncle sighed. "And we don't know who they are or if they're even in Pueblo, but I'll rest easier knowing you're on the case. By the way, ain't nobody seen fit to elect a sheriff in that hellhole, so naturally you'll represent the whole law: local, state and federal."

"Hell, Uncle Mart, this is worse than I thought, but I'll take the damned job."

"Good," his uncle stated.

It was then that Clay's uncle, Major Campton, had introduced him to the new, ready-rolled cigarettes by offering him one. Clay had liked them and managed to take all his uncle had on hand with him to Pueblo. His uncle told him the cigarettes were imported from England, and, since they both liked them, another supply would be obtained and sent to him in Pueblo.

Clay turned from the window, rewrapping the guns and placing them in a drawer along with the packs of cigarettes he had brought with him. He undressed and neatly laid his clothes on a chair, removed his watch chain from his yellow vest and climbed into bed. His body was tired and weary from the long journey from Austin, Texas, through Mexico to Santa Fe and from there by horseback to Pueblo, Colorado.

It was near noon when Clay awoke to the noisy rumbling of wagons and men shouting. He washed and dressed, feeling dull pangs of hunger and remembering his last good meal in Mexico just before crossing over into Colorado. He reached in the drawer for a pack of cigarettes and his guns, but decided not to wear the guns just yet in order to get a better picture of the town.

A small group of cattlemen in the hotel lobby stopped talking as he came down the steps wearing his hickory-striped pants, white shirt with a shoestring tie and yellow vest. Given the heat of the day, he knew his coat would be a burden. They followed him with their eyes until he reached a table in the dining room where he sat ordering his food.

Later, with a full meal under his belt, Clay walked to the street, sizing up the town. Still, men watched him, his fancy attire making quite an impression. What kind of impression, only their minds knew. The sun beat down unmercifully upon the hard-baked streets. Clay chose to walk over to the general store where he leaned against a post, smiling. The boards in the sidewalk plunked and planked according to the men and women passing. All eyes turned for a moment of quick appraisal upon the stranger as they went by. The people of Pueblo had interest in any stranger they saw, for strangers usually meant trouble in one form or another, especially with men like Texas Red Morgan and Blair Tyson running the town as they saw fit. Blair Tyson was a lawyer and his word was law; the free-swinging guns of Texas Red Morgan always backing him up.

About a half an hour went by before Clay left his spot with mental notes of all the people he had seen, their attitudes and general condition. He walked towards the livery stable where he had stabled his horse. His quick eyes, glancing up and into windows along the street, caught sight of folks peeping out from behind curtains. He smiled to himself and thought; "News of a stranger sure gets around fast in this town."

Clay walked through the open door of the livery stable and was met by the keeper, a friendly old man with drooped shoulders.

"That your horse there?"

"Yep. Did he behave all right?" Clay asked.

"I reckon," said the old man. "When I came in this morning he was raising hell, but he settled down once I fed 'em."

"Good, and I thank you. Did you clean him?"

"That I did, mister. Don't usually do that unless I'm asked, but I sorta took to this big fella's coat."

Clay understood that the man was a horse lover, much like himself. He tossed the keeper a few dollars in silver saying, "Thanks. This should take care of him for a month."

"Sure will, mister. I'll take real good care of him. What's his name?"

"Baldy. He flies like an eagle almost," laughed Clay.

Clay led the big red stallion out and mounted. The shinning black saddle, resplendent in white trim, made a striking contrast and added even more splendor to the rider's appearance. Clay rode off with the red horse prancing and feeling frisky, wanting the rider to give him his head.

Out in the open country, passing a few small ranches, Clay rode at his leisure, noticing the beauty of the fertile green stretches of good, rich soil. The air had a pleasant feeling of coolness and far into the distance he could see the painted blue tips of Pike's Peak pointing skyward. It gave him a sense of well-being. In this troubled land a man could find peace away from the noisy town.

A giant forest, green and cool, stood majestically making the earth beneath a soft carpet of lush green. Bits of greasewood and whole patches of cottonwood blended well with the leafy branches. Large birds watched lazily inspecting the lone rider. Clay rode with his mind and eyes alert among the dense cover of bushes.

Within twenty minutes Clay had ridden to the bank of the Arkansas River, its muddy body curving and bending like a giant snake. Further down along the riverbank was a landing where a few barges could be seen. Although the weather was cooler now, he could see the glancing sunrays trying to penetrate the surface, only to be tossed towards the bank.

Here nature was rampant. The river flowed between two shale hills for about two miles; the tops of the hills were flat, where Clay was now sitting and looking at the panorama of the earth and all it had to offer. The smell was fresh. And in the quiet stillness he could hear the leaping of five-pound trout, bass and catfish falling back into the darkness of the river after jumping up to snag a tasty insect, almost daring fishermen to try their luck in catching any of these citizens of the river.

Clay then rode along the river to return to Pueblo by the south end of town since he had ridden out of the north end. This gave him a fairly good layout of the land.

During the time Clay had ridden out of town it was by no mere chance he was being discussed by Texas Red Morgan and his boss, Blair Tyson. Everything about the stranger was being talked over by the two men. The fact that Clay was seen without guns gave Texas Red a sense of indifference.

"Hell, Blair," said Texas Red, "this hombre is just a tin horn gambler, nobody we should worry about."

Blair Tyson listened but by no means was he being taken in by Texas Red's lack of concern. Blair was a lawyer, and a sharp one; he wasn't about to underestimate this stranger.

"We'll see what this gent's all about when he returns from his little ride," said Texas Red, adjusting his two heavy .44 Colts and taking a seat near the open window in Blair's office. From Red's vantage point on the second floor over Miss Ben's Dress Shop, he could see both ends of the town as well as the front of the hotel. "One thing's for sure, Blair," said Texas Red, "if he wants trouble, we can sure as hell give it to him."

Blair laughed at his gunman before dropping his eyes back to his desk to study the papers he'd been working on.

Throughout the town there was talk about the stranger taking place in other quarters. Mr. Phillips looked upon the newcomer with speculation as he talked with Mr. Bryant, the banker. And talk in the dress shop had the women of the town wondering if this handsome stranger had left someone behind. All in all, the townspeople of Pueblo were playing a waiting game. The all waited, wanting to see the stranger's hand.

TWO

Clay finally rode back into town. People along the main street hesitated as he approached and passed. His eyes, keen from experience, caught the hidden eyes watching him.

"Here he comes!" cried Texas Red.

Blair Tyson got up from his desk and walked to the window where Red stood looking out. Their eyes followed Clay all the way up the street until he turned the corner at the north end.

"From his dress, I'd say that gent's definitely a gambler or a ladies' man," declared Red, rising to leave the room.

"Could be. That yellow vest is something," laughed Blair.

"No guns either," answered Red, "unless he's got a hideout like you, Blair." Texas Red laughed out loud as if he held Blair in disdain.

Blair let Red's remark go, but said, "All right. Let's go see what we can find out."

Texas Red led Blair out of the office and down the steps to the street, where he absentmindedly loosened his guns. Both men walked slowly, hoping to get a better look at Clay. Not seeing him, they turned into the Payday Casino where they figured the stranger was bound to show up sooner or later.

Clay, after putting his horse, Baldy, away, traded a few words with the hostler and then returned to the hotel. It was late in the afternoon and he relished the idea of a bath followed by some food.

A few men were in the dining room when he sauntered in and took a seat. The waitress took his order without comment but Clay appreciated her hip movements as she walked away. She knew it and smiled to herself.

Across the room, Mr. Phillips rose from his table and made his way over to Clay, where he addressed the younger man.

"Good evening, sir."

Clay glanced up in acknowledgement and returned, "Yes, it is, but still a little warm."

The two men exchanged smiles.

"May I sit a minute?" asked Mr. Phillips. Then he added, "I heard your name is Clinton."

"Yep, that's me," replied Clay, beginning to get annoyed.

Mr. Phillips noticed his guest while the waitress returned and placed Clay's meal on the table before him.

"We have right nice meals here, Mr. Clinton."

"I take it you are Mr. Phillips?"

The older man leaned back with pride. "That's right, son. And before we go any further, I want to share some advice."

Clay looked up, trying to figure the man's move. "It's a free country. What's on your mind?"

Mr. Phillips grunted and leaned forward. "Son, I've seen men come and go in this town, and I figure I've got a right to judge the men I see."

"I see," Clay laughed, "what's that got to do with me?"

"Now, mind you son, listen close. I've got a friend I wrote to some time ago, a Major Campton in Austin, and in the letter I asked him for some help in cleaning up this town. He said he'd send a man..."

"Well," said Clay, cursing his uncle under his breath.

The old man continued, "Well, I'd stake a handsome lot that you're that man."

Clay finished chewing the last bite of his food and took from his pocket the package of cigarettes, offering one to Mr. Phillips.

The old man looked at the brown, rolled objects and said, "What's this?"

Clay laughed. "They're ready-rolled cigarettes."

"Well, I'll be. What in tarnation will they think up next?" Phillips lit the cigarette, just as Clay did, and puffed, savoring the new idea in smoking.

Clay watched Mr. Phillips with mild curiosity. Feeling he could trust the man he said, "Major Campton is my uncle."

Upon hearing this, Mr. Phillips relaxed, his face showing both strain and eagerness in telling Clay that he was being run wide open by Blair Tyson and his gunman, Texas Red Morgan.

Clay listened without interruption while Mr. Phillips declared, "These men have a gang of gunmen who do their bidding. Not long ago they took a young girl from the Payday Casino and, naturally, they used her up. I saw this man, Red, kill three men with my own eyes, and one was the sheriff we'd elected. Clinton, we need help."

"Call me Clay, Mr. Phillips."

"All right, Clay. I have a daughter. She's only twenty-one and by God these skunks look at her with ideas. Nothing's happened to her so far, but if one of those bastards were to lay a hand on her, I'd kill him. I had to tell Texas Red that, and Tyson gave him the word to lay off." He stopped talking and sighed. "I wish Pet, that's my daughter, had a mother. Clay, she's a sweet girl, but she's headstrong and as spirited as a wild stallion. I sure hope you can give me hand."

Clay's face became serious. He rose from the table before saying, "Listen, Mr. Phillips, I'll see what I can do to help."

Mr. Phillips extended his hand, and noticing that Clay wore no guns said, "Clay, what was your uncle thinking when he sent you out here? Hell, I asked him to send a marshal or a ranger, not an investigator or an observer to report back. We need a man on the job now!"

Clay let a deep smile cross his face at the older man's surmising and then said, "Don't worry, Mr. Phillips, you got all you asked for, believe me."

Both men extended hands and shook as Clay said, "Keep our talk quiet, even from your daughter, till you hear different from me." With that said, he walked out.

The sun was setting, casting a golden glow mixed with red. The air felt like rain but the cloudless sky reflected only blue. Clay stood for a minute, then moved off towards the Payday Casino.

Blair Tyson and Texas Red Morgan were still in the

Payday when Clay walked in and stopped at the bar. Blair and Red tossed an inquiring look. The bartender uttered, "Whatta'ya have?"

"Brandy," Clay answered, watching the people in the saloon in the mirror behind the bar that gave him a clear view of the entire room as well as its occupants.

A crowd of men surrounded a gambling table, while a couple of girls working in the saloon for Kate, sat at a table feasting their eyes on Clay. Kate herself saw Clay come in and was surprised. She smoothed the front of her dress and smiled at the girls sitting with her. The watched as Kate got up and approached Clay.

Just as the bartender sat Clay's brandy before him, she smiled and said, "That's on the house, Sam." Kate stood looking at Clay. "It's been a long time, friend."

"Sure has, Kate, but you haven't changed a bit."

Kate took Clay's drink and led him to a table where they continued to talk. Kate was a well-built woman of thirty-two, the same age as Clay. Her jet-black hair went well with her sparkling green eyes; and even though she had had a harsh life, there were no signs of it in her face or in her manners. Her figure was that of a young maiden and men still turned to look at her when she walked by. She used a costly perfume, and in the business of running a saloon this made her an enhancement to the trade.

The last time Clay had seen Kate was about five years back, when they both had been in California. Kate never knew Clay was a lawman, but often suspected such. She remembered the time Clay had rescued her from a bunch of saddle tramps. Since that time, they'd become good friends. She'd never asked him about himself, being satisfied with what he volunteered to tell her about his personal life.

Blair Tyson let a sneer turn into a leering smile as he watched Kate making small talk with Clay. Not that Kate was his woman, but he hated the idea of Kate spending time with the stranger.

"Told you he was a ladies' man," Texas Red remarked.

"Take it easy, Red. If Kate knows him, I'll find out about him and what business he's got here in Pueblo."

"Texas Red laughed, "Better say you reckon you will."

Texas Red could see Blair wasn't enjoying the scene. He stood and loosened his guns. Blair got up and followed him towards the table where Kate and Clay were sitting. Texas Red took up a new position against the bar as Blair stood at Clay's table speaking words to Kate but looking at Clay.

"Hello, Kate," he remarked.

"Hi, Blair," she returned as she looked up before returning her eyes to Clay.

"Looks like old home week," teased Blair.

No one spoke. Finally, Clay looked at Blair with a cold, impersonal stare. Kate spoke up quickly, "Yeah, sort of."

The entire room seemed to quiet down. All eyes were glued on the table where Blair Tyson was holding forth. Clay figured Blair out, and, for the moment, disbanded Texas Red from his mind.

"I didn't catch your name, mister," said Blair Tyson, beginning to feel the coldness of Clay Clinton.

"That's because I didn't toss it in your direction," answered Clay.

"No, I guess you didn't toss it my way," said Blair

as his face reddened at this affront.

Texas Red relaxed a little when Blair said to Clay, "I'll see you around."

Clay never answered, never showed any signs of being bothered or that he had even heard Blair's remark.

When Blair and Texas Red moved away, Kate laid her hand on Clay's arm and smiled as she said, "Watch those two. You've seen nothing like them before."

This was a sincere warning. Kate knew the fact that Clay wasn't carrying a gun would make no difference to Texas Red.

Clay looked at the woman and replied, "Thanks, Kate."

Kate's smile vanished as she said, "Clay, this town is hell. You'll see. And there's nothing anyone can do." Then she told him how wide open the town was and how Billy Ferrell was walking around town scot-free after killing old Tom Johnson. "He shot him in the back, Clay. It was cold-blooded murder."

"From what I understand, isn't Blair the law?"

She laughed. "Law? Tom Johnson was the law, Clay. The one who got shot and it happened right here. Billy is one of Blair's men."

"What did the townsfolk do?"

Are you kidding? Buck Blair Tyson and you face his nine gunmen. One is bound to get you."

Clay realized that Kate was telling him exactly what Mr. Phillips had told him earlier that evening. He reached for his cigarettes and offered Kate one. She was so amazed at the new ready-rolled cigarettes Clay gave her the pack that he had with him.

"Thanks, Clay, the girls will help me smoke these."

"Kate, why did you tell me about the town troubles?"

She laughed. "I wonder myself. But your work always seems to be headed in trouble's direction. Of course I could be wrong, but I always pegged you for a lawman of some sort. Now you take that time in..."

Clay cut her short and leaving her at the table, he walked to the bar for another drink and heard the delighted squeals coming from the girls where Kate was passing out the new type of cigarettes. Clay watched them acting like children over a tasty piece of candy.

He was about to leave when a loud noise attracted his attention towards the front door. He heard the repeated shots of a few guns and had started toward the sound when through the front door rode a cowboy brandishing a gun.

"All right," yelled the rider, "I'm back! Gimme a drink, hell, gimme the whole bottle!"

With this the rider slammed a couple of shots through the bar, then slid out of the saddle. The crowd in the Payday had seen this before and knew this sort of action might end up with a slug in anyone present. But, as usual, they hesitated to do anything about it.

Kate walked over to the rider and shouted, "All right, Billy. I told you not to bring this damn horse in here!"

The rider, mean and surly, smiled a crooked smile.

"Kate, you know my horse goes wherever I go. Hell, this ol' horse is better than some of these folks you serve. Now shut up and give me a drink. Or would you rather see my horse do a dance?"

Kate nodded to Sam the bartender to give the rider a bottle. She remembered the last time Billy made his horse dance. It almost wrecked the place.

"Pay up, Billy, and get out!!" demanded Kate.

"Not so fast, Kate. You know I'm a slow-drinking man."

Clay let his eyes bore a hole into the rider as his own muscles flexed. He clenched his fists. Billy's eyes found Clay's.

"You don't seem to relish me and my horse in here, do you?"

Clay was aware of the nasty situation facing him and also noticed that Blair and Texas Red had returned.

"The lady said get out."

"Now ain't that something. The lady said get out," sneered Billy.

"Not only that, but I say the same."

Billy's eyes narrowed. He still held a gun in one hand. Texas Red started forward, but Blair held him back. Then, without saying a word, Clay took the horse's bridle and led him out the door. As he returned, Billy had his gun leveled at Clay's middle.

Clay walked up to him and said, "Now, I suggest you follow your horse. Or do they carry you out?"

Billy laughed and for a second his face relaxed and his gun lowered. This was the cold, calculated second Clay had been waiting for. With catlike quickness, Clay moved inside Billy's gun arm, pushed it aside and placed a murderous fist into the pit of Billy's gut. His punch made the man double over and Clay brought his left hand down hard behind Billy's neck. Billy dropped to the floor like a folded ox and lay still.

Directing his eyes to Kate, Clay said, "Get somebody to drag him out."

Kate was astonished at what had happened, but was

a little leery of Blair and Texas Red. She stepped up and called two men to do her bidding.

Texas Red challenged Clay, "You put him there, fancy vest, you take him out."

"I only put them there, I don't move them," Clay said matter-of-factly.

Texas Red was about to carry on when Blair moved in between the two men. Blair was cool and calm when he spoke.

"Take him down to jail, Red. Get those saddle punks to help you."

Clay stood with his back to the bar as the three men struggled with the dead weight of Billy Ferrell.

Blair ordered Kate, "Get me a drink." As she went behind the bar to pour a drink, Blair spoke to Clay. "I see you don't like this town, mister. Either that, or you just don't want to live long." Kate returned with Blair's drink just in time to hear his last remark.

Clay recognized the threat and said, "I don't scare easy and I intend to stay here in Pueblo for quite a while."

"We don't like strangers butting into our business around here."

"Are you the law?" asked Clay, feeling for his cigarettes and remembering he had given the pack to Kate.

"Yeah, now that you ask, we don't have what you'd call a lawman... but my word is law around here."

"Oh, I see. And you permit horses and riders to dirty up public places?" Clay asked pointing to the manure on the floor.

Blair looked at the pile and laughed, "Billy was only having a little fun. Hell, we're entitled to that."

"I don't call it fun, nor does the lady here."

"Shoot, Kate understands how Billy feels about his horse."

Clay became annoyed with Blair. Staring hard he said, "If I'm around and he does it again, it might not be just a trip to jail. If he's a friend of yours, you might want to warn him."

Before Blair could answer, Clay walked out saying, "Goodnight, Kate."

Blair let loose at Kate as Clay left. "Seems to me he's more than a mere friend."

"Well he isn't. But even if he was, it's none of your business," Kate said as she strolled away.

The crowd became alive again. The whole scene displeased Blair and he quickly rushed out to find Texas Red.

On the street the sun was down and darkness painted the night. The stars were out in fine array and the moon seemed to be smiling in its crescent shape. Horses were tied to the hitching rails, and the town had begun its night's task of merriment. A cool wind whipped the down the street, leaving a fine layer of dust on everything it touched. Folks walking through town were rapidly dusting themselves off.

Clay walked up the street thinking of the run in he'd had with Blair and his men. To him, it was good. Further down the street he had to move from the sidewalk as another cowpoke had chosen to ride his horse down the wooden walk. Clay began to realize the vastness of the job he had been sent to do.

The news of his exploit of knocking Billy Ferrell down preceded him. Men passed and nodded as if they were pleased. Clay decided he was going to get a full view of the town in this one night; and it wasn't even nine o'clock yet. He walked between the two buildings with almost flat roofs, storing every detail in his mind. He walked and stopped to listen, his keen ears detecting footsteps. Someone was following him. From the shape and size of the building that he was in back of, he knew it was the hotel. Clay moved slowly up the alley, then around a corner, and waited.

The follower still came. Clay raised his fist as a shadow came into view. He stepped out, throwing his right hand and catching the follower squarely on the chin. The shadow moaned and fell to the ground with a thud. Realizing this person may have a gun; Clay checked the hands first, and then bent over to see who was so interested in his movements. He turned the body over and discovered it was a girl.

The blond hair glistened from her head, free from the hat that now lay a good foot away. Her breasts were heavy with unconscious breathing. Then he noticed the gun belt with its weapon still in the holster and thought, "Who in the hell could this be." He lifted the gun and saw it was a .38. He put it in his pocket and began slapping her face gently until she stirred. Then he moved off into the alley and took a position on the main street to watch the girl as she became conscious. He was sure she couldn't recognize him; otherwise she wouldn't have tried to follow him.

He didn't have long to wait before the girl, wearing black boots with faded Levis tucked into them, stumble from between the buildings to the main street. There was enough light to see her dismay at the empty holster. She carried her hat, letting her blond hair flow down her shoulders. Clay smiled to himself, but still felt puzzled. The girl mopped at her face, looking to see if there was any blood. She looked up and down the street, then walked over to a little painted mare, untied her and led the horse up the street toward the stable.

Clay kept in the shadows and watched as she entered the livery stable and shortly returned. She continued down the street alone and turned into the hotel. Clay followed and waited across the street in front of the general store to see if she would come out again. Presently, he saw a light being lit and a shade being drawn partly down. Again he glanced up at the lighted window and saw a shadowy movement on the roof of the building next to the hotel. Clay's mind quickly went over the hotel's layout and decided this lighted room was just up the hall from his own, with the window facing the building next door instead of the street.

Clay hurried through the alley again, realizing what the shadow he saw meant. He could see no way up to the roof, but took out the .38 as he heard movement, then saw the shadow again. He fired and the shadow fled into the night across the rooftops. Clay thought, "You'll be back, mister... and I'll be waiting."

THREE

Clay lay in bed, smoking and thinking about the events of his first day in Pueblo. He knew just what had to be done. The incident last night in the alley gave him a queer feeling, yet he wasn't quite sure how to handle this girl.

Clay glanced at the chair where the confiscated .38 pistol lay and decided he would give the gun back. After a great deal of contemplation, he figured the girl had to be Mr. Phillips' daughter, Pet. Yet he pondered. "Why in the hell would she be following me?" He would talk to Mr. Phillips and find out all he knew. With his plans now formed for the following day, Clay tossed a few times before dropping off to sleep.

Bright and early the next morning Clay was up and had decided it still wasn't the right time to declare himself. After dressing and putting two packs of the ready-rolled cigarettes in his pockets, he went downstairs. He had not forgotten the girl and the gun, and felt awkward having it in his pocket.

Clay was eating when Mr. Phillips came into the dining room. He looked up and beckoned to the older man. They exchanged morning greetings as Mr.

Phillips sat down and ordered breakfast for himself. Clay could see a worried expression on the man's face, and knew instantly that his hunch about the identity of the girl with the gun was right. He inquired, "Does your daughter have breakfast early, Mr. Phillips?"

"Usually she does, but she's not feeling well this morning."

Clay had to smile, thinking to himself, "I guess not after last night's events."

"What's the trouble?"

"Well, last night she went to her room and before she put out the lights she said she saw a figure of a man across the alley on the next roof. I told her maybe it was her imagination." He paused and sighed deeply before continuing. "Anyway, she took it upon herself to investigate it. She said she followed the man into the back alley where he knocked her down and took her gun."

Clay knew what the girl had seen, and realized now that she had mistaken him for the Peeping Tom. He laughed and produced the .38, asking, "Is this your daughter's gun?"

"Yes. But how did you get it?" Mr. Phillips asked in surprise.

Clay explained the events of the previous night, including the part about Billy Ferrell and ended by saying, "I caught whoever was following me from a corner. I'm sorry it was your daughter I knocked unconscious." He didn't mention seeing a figure on the roof and firing a shot in that direction. He didn't want to worry the older man any further.

"I'll wait until later on in the day to give your daughter her gun back," he said jokingly.

Mr. Phillips seemed pleased and even laughed about the unintentional punch Clay had given Pet. They talked some more and Mr. Phillips asked for one of those new kind of rolls. Clay gave him a pack and said, "Keep them, I'll be getting more soon."

In his conversation with Mr. Phillips Clay learned he had a small herd of dairy cows west of town and that he sold milk, butter, cheese and eggs to folks in town. In addition, he also shipped some to the mining town of Leadville and to Denver. Mr. Phillips explained that his dairy, which was a new thing, was on the verge of expanding according to the growth of Pueblo. With the railroad running from Pueblo to Denver and Leadville, he was thinking of enlarging his herd from fifty cows to at least a hundred or so. He revealed the cost to Clay and Clay became genuinely interested when Mr. Phillips made him an offer to come into the business. As Clay listened, he saw the importance of the dairy in this part of the country and the large market there was available. It became apparent then that the town of Pueblo had to be cleaned up. He decided to spend the day riding west and east of town since he'd spent the day before on the north and south ends of town.

Presently, the men ended their conversation and separated, Mr. Phillips going toward the bank and Clay moving off toward the livery stable, where he talked a while with the hostler as he saddled up Baldy and rode off.

Blair Tyson, Texas Red Morgan and Billy Ferrell were coming out of the building that served as a jail. It had at least three cells, and next to them was a large storeroom where Blair's men kept their gear. The sun was up and the day was beginning to warm up degree by degree. The men walked abreast on the sidewalk, causing people to step into the street to walk around them. The three continued on to Blair's office.

Texas Red spoke up, "Listen, Blair, I still say shoot the bastard and we'll have no headaches."

Blair tilted his hat. "No, not until he shows his hand. Then, Red, the pleasure is all yours."

"I want to do the job, Blair," Billy Ferrell interrupted.

All remained quiet until Blair said, "No, Billy, we need you to take care of the other job. Now get on out to that spread of Phillips and take care of business. Then go to Leadville and bring Hank back with you."

Texas Red started to protest, but Blake pulled him short. "I have my mind made up. We get Phillips' place first, then we go back to that last job in Denver. Hell, boys, we've got enough to last us until this job comes off."

Billy Ferrell stormed from the room saying; "I'll see you in about a week."

"Do you really think knocking off that bull of Phillips' will help?" Red asked.

"Hell yes. If he can't keep his cows fresh, he can't produce milk. My God, what a gold mine."

"Yeah, Phillips was sure long-sighted," remarked Texas Red.

Blair Tyson walked over to the window and looked out. He turned to Texas Red and ordered; "Red, you go over to the line shack and give Tim his money. And," he added, "tell them all to be in town Friday night."

Texas Red Morgan left Blair alone. He drew his riding gloves and put them on. Red smiled as he thought about last night's events. A crazy pleasure assailed him as he became stimulated from the thoughts. He walked up the street, bumping into people without even noticing them. At the livery stable he saddled his horse and rode off without saying a word to the holster.

Clay had taken his time riding out to the Phillips' dairy ranch. He was studying the surrounding landscape, noticing the few trail crossings and even venturing to explore them for a mile or so to be sure of the land and to get his bearings. At the edge of the clearing Clay sat looking at the well laid out arrangement of the dairy ranch; the whitewashed fences and barn, the milling herd out in the pasture and the little stream that flowed near the spring house. The white clapboard house, with its flowers and garden, pleased him.

Clay heard the sound of laughter and reached for his binoculars in the saddlebags. Putting the glasses to his eyes, he brought them around to see a few men standing near a big Jersey bull that was pawing and snorting. The men seemed to be teasing the bull. He then saw the reason for their laughter. A ranch hand was holding a heifer to be mated by the bull but upon the bull mounting, the heifer would step away.

Clay saw the blond hair of Pet, hanging down to her shoulders as it was the previous night, emerge from the house in full stride and yelling, "Hold her still, Walt."

The men continued laughing.

The girl waited until the bull was again in position, and noticed the trouble: the cow was built too low. She cast a few angry glances at the laughing men, who stopped their foolishness when they saw the look on her face. The girl walked up beside the bull and without hesitation seized the situation and, with her hand, guided the bull into service.

She turned again to the men. "How would you feel in a like state?"

None of the hired hands answered, they just dropped their heads and went about their work.

Clay laughed to himself and thought, "What a woman." He admired her hearty courage and was pleased that she wasn't a squeamish female. Through the glasses he watched the even movement of her wide hips as she returned to the house. He could see the slight bounce of her breasts. He liked everything about her except the fact that she wore blue jeans and a gun belt. He noticed she had another gun jammed in her holster. "Damn," he muttered.

The men who had watched the service of the bull evidently returned to other chores, they had all disappeared. Clay replaced his binoculars and started out of his hiding place. Just then he heard the echo of a shot explode through the air. He looked toward the sound and saw a faint swirl of smoke. Then he heard a horse traveling hell-bent for leather.

Clay heeled Baldy and the horse jumped forward in the direction of the sound. Carefully he looked around on foot, where he read signs of a man having been in the grass maybe twenty-five yards from where the shot had been fired. The grass was just springing back into place. He kneeled and picked up a spent shell that was lying near his feet. He examined it and saw it was a .44-.70. It came from a heavy gun, maybe an Arnold Sharp's rifle or a buffalo gun.

With slow strides Clay returned to his horse and

rode towards the ranch, approaching it from the south. A shot whizzed by his head and he heard a command, "Stop, right there!"

Clay reigned up. He could see who was on the other end of the .30-.30. She moved out in front of him, still holding the rifle at his middle. "Who are you and what the hell are you doing on this range?"

Clay looked at Pet and saw that she meant business. "I was riding by and heard a shot."

"Get off that horse."

He slid from the saddle as the girl shouted, "Pete, get that rifle from his boot."

It was then Clay saw the men, and not a friendly face among them. The man called Pete removed Clay's rifle and smelled the barrel. "It ain't been fired in a month of Sundays, Pet."

Pet looked at this man wearing the bright yellow vest and felt a strange feeling, one of fear and reproach. She felt she was being drawn to this tall stranger in a way that caused her face to redden. She knew he was looking through her, yet she felt powerless to avert his eyes on his mind. Pet knew within her, for some strange reason - stranger than herself - that this man was her biggest threat. She mustered all her strength to fight against it, knowing all along she would be glad to lose the battle and not be ashamed.

Clay reasoned that Pet was honest in her purpose, and although she was strong-willed, he could sense her fury building up against him. He broke the silence by asking, "Just who were you looking for?"

She dropped her lip and stood back on her well-developed legs. "Some punk just shot our bull."

"And you thought it was me?"

"Just how am I supposed to know that it wasn't, mister?"

"Listen, call me Clay." He handed her the spent shell saying, "Know anybody who carries a .44-.70?"

Pet asked the men around her, but no one could come up with an answer.

"Come over here a second," Pet motioned to Clay.

Clay trailed her, ever mindful of her curves. He also remembered the punch and her gun. Pet took him over to where the bull lay. He could see that she was hurt, but knew she wouldn't cry, at least not in front of him.

"It's a damn shame!" she exclaimed.

"Who would do it?" Clay asked thoughtfully.

"That's what I'd like to know. But wait till Dad hears about it; he'll go hog wild." Pet returned the spent .44-.70 shell to Clay and started toward the house.

"Just a minute."

His voice startled her and as she turned around Clay extended his hand, holding the .38. "I think this is yours."

He saw the rage in her eyes flare up and with a hate-filled twist to her lips she growled, "How in the hell did you get that?"

He became serious as he looked into her eyes saying steadily, "You should know."

She started to speak, but his words prevented her.

"I don't take to people following me, especially in a dark alley."

"You should at least apologize for hitting a woman; you could have broken my face."

Clay felt a bit relieved, but knew he was in for a sound cursing out. Yet he figured even that would be kind of nice coming from Pet. "Yeah, I could have and you could have gotten killed, but luckily I wasn't wearing a gun at the time."

She looked at him with a cold and impersonal stare. "Who are you?"

"I told you, call me Clay. And as for any apology for hitting a woman, it wouldn't have happened if you'd have stayed in a woman's place."

She was furious. "Damn you and a woman's place. I try to get to the bottom of anything that concerns me. It certainly wasn't any of your business."

"I think it was."

Pet, still holding her returned .38, asked, "Is there anything else you want around here? If not, please leave."

He looked at her, and with his eyes undressed her. And she felt it. Clay was trying to shame her into gentleness, but it didn't work.

She arched her brows and replied with fire, "That, you'll never have."

Clay walked away from her and mounted his horse. On the way out he rode past her and said, "Maybe I'll never be able to have it, but take some advice from me and keep the shades down. That fellow who's been trying to peep at it may decide to go further."

She realized he knew why she was following him, and now understood he had actually mistaken him for the same man, or at least some other man. Nevertheless, it didn't stop her hot words, "Damn you, you know way too much."

FOUR

Clay rode back into Pueblo. After returning Baldy to the livery stable, he hurried over to the station where he stood until the 4:25 train arrived. He then sent a wire to his uncle in Texas. He stopped at the hotel on the way back and had something to eat. Having finished his meal, Clay went to his room, washed and changed clothes, putting on a blue shirt and a pair of gray trousers. He also changed hats from the dark, dirty brown one to a white Stetson. His thought now was to see Mr. Phillips.

Returning downstairs, he took a chair on the hotel porch and waited for his man. Up the street he saw one of the girls from Kate Murphy's Payday Casino being roped by a cowpuncher. The girl was screaming as the cowpoke pulled her along behind his horse. Clay heard a woman comment, "It's shameful. A woman can't even walk down the street." He noticed the people seemed concerned, but no one ventured forth to help. Clay stepped out into the street and swiftly grabbed the horse's bridle. The man was surprised and shouted, "Turn my horse loose!"

"Not until you unrope the girl."

"Just having fun. Didn't know she was your mother, mister."

Hearing this, Clay released the bridle and with the swiftness of a cobra snatched the rider from the saddle and sank his fist solidly into his mouth. The man cursed and fell, and, in doing so, made a play for his gun. Clay dived as the gun roared. He put both hands around the cowpunchers throat and squeezed. Clay saw the contorted look on the man's face and said slowly, "Drop it."

Clay felt the man's hands grip his wrists, so he applied more pressure until the hands dropped away. Rising to his feet, he looked at the sobbing cowpuncher and said, "Somebody bring some water." The man's gun was tossed aside. When an elderly man handed Clay a pail full of water, he poured it in the cowpuncher's face before walking away.

Clay could hear the man cursing, and the people who had seen the scuffle had disbanded just as quickly as they had gathered. He brushed off his dust-covered clothes and again took his seat on the hotel porch.

Mr. Phillips had seen Clay from his window and hurried over. He saw Clay sitting there as if nothing had happened.

Seeing Mr. Phillips, Clay said, "You're just the man I wanted to see."

Mr. Phillips took a chair beside his young friend. Clay told him about the bull and all about his meeting with Pet. Mr. Phillips took it all in with calm expression, but Clay knew it was a bluff and asked, "Have you any ideas on it?"

It was then Mr. Phillips told him that the ranch wasn't mortgaged and that Blair Tyson had offered him ten thousand in cash for half interest. After swatting a fly Mr. Phillips continued, "Blair came to this town years ago a gambling lawyer, and by God he didn't do enough business to have ten thousand in cash on hand."

"Do you think he could have been trying to buy a share of your ranch for someone else?"

"No, not Blair, he wants it all for himself. They laughed at me when I first started, but now they all see the possibilities of the dairy and they want in. Now I'll have to mortgage something in order to buy another god bull and stay in business."

"You just let me know if anyone offers to help you with the money. Butcher the old bull and just say he wasn't doing a good job. That way we might flush the interested party out into the open."

After Mr. Phillips agreed, Clay asked, "By the way, do you know anyone who owns a .44-.70 Sharpe?"

The kindly old man thought for a moment then, rising to his feet, shouted, "Hell, yes, I know one... Billy Ferrell. But he rode out of town right after you did."

Clay, satisfied that he'd discovered the identity of the man who shot the bull, decided to keep the spent shell to prove his case.

Mr. Phillips became apprehensive. He knew now that Blair Tyson was behind the killing of his bull. He would have to have money to buy another and he, having no alternative, would let Blair Tyson buy in as a partner of the dairy ranch. Clay had thought about this too, and was glad to learn about Tyson's condition when he'd first come to Pueblo. He wondered how Tyson was making his money. He knew for a fact that Texas Red wasn't hanging around for free. Texas Red was a paid killer, and from what Phillips had said, there were eight more on Blair's payroll.

To give Mr. Phillips assurance, Clay let him know that within a few days he would begin to see some changes in Pueblo, in particular, the U.S. Marshal's star. Mr. Phillips was pleased with the news.

After a bit Clay looked up and saw two women coming toward the hotel. He stared eagerly as they approached and entered. Amazed by their beauty, Clay whispered to his friend, "Who are they – wasn't one a Negro woman?"

"That's Madam LaCall and her maid. She owns the bonnet and dress shop next to Kate's place." Mr. Phillips added, "That's one handsome Negro girl."

Clay nodded, still somewhat puzzled.

"They always take their meals here in the evening," Mr. Phillips informed him.

"Oh, I see," stammered Clay.

Mr. Phillips slapped at his arm, missing the fly. Then he said, "Sometimes a Negro or ramrodder comes through, but nothing ever happens. Guess folks don't notice the color unless attention is brought to it."

"That's the best damn thing I've heard about this town," ventured Clay.

Both men continued sitting on the hotel porch. When Madam LaCall and her maid came out again, Clay looked at the striking beauty of the Negro girl. "Beautiful and young," he thought. "I've seen quite a few Negroes and quadroons, but that one is a beauty," he said aloud.

Mr. Phillips nodded in agreement. "Clay, you seem to be a tolerant man. Any particular reason?"

"Yes and no. I just don't like to see anyone taken

advantage of, and, I appreciate and can admire a man of any race – if he's a man of his word and a man of character."

Mr. Phillips was the first to get up saying, "Well, I've got to see about getting some food. Have you eaten yet?"

"Go ahead, I've had mine."

"Thanks, Clay, for taking care of things for me, son. I just hope this bunch of snakes makes your work light."

"They won't," Clay laughed.

Again night had fallen on Pueblo. The temperature cooled as the town, weary from the cares of the day, settled down. Gigantic clouds floated aimlessly by the moon. The shadows from the buildings appeared like a haunting and elusive dream. Clay could smell the salty aroma of animal sweat mixed with a sharp scent of green pines and spruce. Even a faint smell of earth found its way into his nostril. He had gone to his room and was looking out the window when Pet rode up, sliding from the saddle before the little mare had even stopped. She tossed the lines over the hitching rail and bounded up the steps of the hotel. Her father listened as she told him of the day's happenings out at the ranch.

She was surprised when he said calmly, "Yes, I know, Pet."

As Mr. Phillips began explaining that Clay had told him all about it, Pet dropped her lip and declared hotly, "I didn't know you would be that interested in a man who beats women."

"Well, after all, dear, you didn't have any business being in that alley."

"But I was... Well, frankly, I don't trust that fancy yellow-vested hound."

"I do, Pet."

"That's just fine, Father, but I don't have to. Do you even know who he is or anything about him?"

"I don't particularly need to know. But I'll tell you one thing: he's a real man."

Pet was aware of it, as she remembered Clay's eyes upon her. "A man, yeah, but what's he after, snooping around our place?"

"He wasn't snooping..." Mr. Phillips, realizing his daughter had met her match in Clay, changed direction; "Now mind you, Pet, Clay won't stand for any of your usual foolishness."

"He what!" Pet roared. "Oh please, don't be a fool. He's just like all the others, looking to use a woman for whatever he can get from her," she said before jumping up to leave.

"Where the devil are you going, young lady?"

"Down to see Kate."

"That girl!" Mr. Phillips exclaimed aloud.

Mr. Phillips knew when Pet visited Kate they always went upstairs to Kate's room. He was glad that she wouldn't allow Pet to hang around the bar. And, indeed, Kate was one of the women who could talk to Pet on her own terms. In Kate, Pet found confidence and friendship. Kate was a counselor to Pet. She could talk to her, help guide her form the pitfalls of life. He knew that Kate loved Pet and that Pet would listen to her.

In the Payday Casino, one of the girls looked up to see Pet strolling into the building wearing her .38, which accentuated her well-formed hips. The hard eyes of the saloon gentry gazed at her with lust and personal ideas of conquest. Even the town boss, Blair

Tyson, was intense in his look before turning back to his hand of poker.

"Kate, here comes your adopted daughter," said one of the girls.

Kate asked one of the girls to take over for a while. Pet paused long enough to greet all the girls she knew. Although they were in that questionable profession, Pet realized they had to make a living and wasn't at all judgmental. It didn't bother her a bit, for through Kate those things and the reasons behind them were all explained.

"Well, baby, you look all in," remarked Kate.

Pet smiled and pouted. Kate placed her arm around her waist and led her upstairs to her two-room apartment. Pet removed her gun belt and boots before curling up in a chair. She unbuttoned her blouse, loosened the belt of her jeans and began to relax in complete comfort.

Kate looked at Pet, noticing her state of undress. She marveled at Pet's virgin body, and was doing all in her power to keep her that way until she met the certain man who wouldn't just spoil it for his own pleasures.

"Pet, why don't you wear that brassiere I gave you?" Kate inquired.

"I don't like it. It makes me conscious of myself."

Kate laughed, but saw the faraway look in Pet's eyes and asked, "Well, what's on that mind of yours?"

"Kate, I saw a man; in fact, I met a man today who scared the hell out of me."

"What's so strange about that? Half the men around here scare me."

"You don't understand, Kate. This is different."

Pet pouted, then revealed to Kate what had happened last night and about the meeting with Clay earlier in the day.

Kate asked, "Is it Clay you're afraid of?"

"Yes I am."

"Why, he's a nice fellow," Kate said warmly.

Pet stood up with a nervous gesture and extended her arms, causing her blouse to flutter against her chest, her breasts partly exposed. "Kate, do you know anything about Clay? Who is he?"

From Pet's questions Kate was beginning to understand what the girl was so afraid of.

"Pet, I knew Clay a good while back in California and believe me, he's a great guy. Why, I know women who would rub their breasts on a cactus just to have him."

"Hell, Kate, he can't be such a good man. He's a woman beater... and I think he's a gambler, too."

"I see you don't know Clay at all. He's got you fooled completely," laughed Kate.

"Aw, just look at how he dresses. Like a ladies' man, like one of those other kind you told me about – you know, one of those men who talk..."

"Listen, baby," Kate cut in, "throw it out of your mind. Clay is a man, every inch of him. It's too damned bad we're only good friends," Kate ended dreamily.

"You mean that you could go for this fancy dressed woman-beater?"

"In a big way. But he's only a man for business. Very few women can say they know him in that sense, and I wish I could be or could have been one of them."

Pet sat on Kate's bed, her blouse falling to one side, completely exposing her firm breast. Kate looked at her with a longing that had been present ever since she'd met the young girl. For Pet was only twenty-one and a virgin, green as grass. Kate knew she had to master her self-control.

Pet suddenly asked, "Kate, how do you feel when you know a man is undressing you and actually playing with you with his eyes?"

Kate laughed as she remembered the first fellow she had fallen in love with. She was certain now that Pet had deep feelings for Clay and that her mixed emotions were leading to her indecision.

Kate answered, "Well, baby, that all depends upon the man. From certain gents it's a hell of a compliment; from others it's flattery; and from still others it'd be a hell of an insult. All in all, it depends on what you think of the man."

"I don't know what to think, to tell the truth. I'd die if anybody knew this, but I can tell you, Kate." Pet fell into silence.

"Well, tell me. You're making me feel as anxious as yourself. And at my age!"

Kate sat on the bed beside Pet and put her arms around her. Pet leaned her head on Kate's large breast and said, "Kate, I felt myself enjoying Clay eyeing me that way. I tried to fight it saying I hate him. But then I kept telling myself, 'He's going to get me sure as hell.' That's the very thing I told myself when I saw him, Kate; 'He's going to get me.' What's more I..."

Kate's arm touched Pet and she shivered. Kate began caressing Pet's body to calm her, feeling to see if Pet's reactions were sensitive. Pet trembled. Kate knew the girl's desires were raging. Kate felt herself losing control.

"Pet, baby, I can tell you this: You've got it bad. You really want this man to have you, don't you?"

Pet didn't answer, so Kate added another question. "Don't you want to give Clay your body? You can actually feel him now, can't you?"

Pet answered through tears, "My God, Kate, is it wrong? I can't help it. And not knowing how, I'm afraid."

Kate couldn't resist Pet any longer. She laid Pet back on the bed and lay down beside her. When Pet turned in towards her, she kissed her and the girl trembled as she cuddled with her.

Pet then threw her arms around Kate and cried, "Kate, please do something for me. Help me. I'm going out of my mind. I feel like I'm on fire and I'm aching. Kate ... My God ... Kate ... Ka ... Kate..."

Kate couldn't fight the girl's pleading. She kissed her again and their passions heightened. She straightened abruptly and said, "You make me want to love you and it's wrong."

"I don't care," exclaimed Pet.

Kate battled with her great passion and desire for Pet. She couldn't Kate's body, in the next second after Pet's, followed course. She felt her own body quiver and shake and she squeezed Pet hard with trembling fingers that slid from the young girl's body. Kate kissed her again and reeled over to one side and onto the floor from the force of her own release. Kate fought and brought herself back to consciousness. She looked at Pet, who was as still as death but smiling as if heaven itself had blessed her. Kate couldn't resist the last kiss of Pet's body and as she did, a second force greater than the first tore her asunder, and she lay with her head on Pet's stomach, crying.

Pet opened her eyes, saw the scene before her and gently lifted Kate's head. Then Kate opened her eyes. Neither spoke. There was nothing to say. Both women stood up and turned their backs to each other in shame and disgrace from their actions. Pet dressed herself. Kate's condition called for an entire change of clothes. When Kate returned from the other room, Pet was standing by the door. They exchanged a fleeting glance.

Finally Kate broke the silence. "I'm a rotten, evil woman, Pet."

"No, no, I'm to blame."

Again they looked at each other. Pet moved to Kate and threw her arms around her. Kate cried, "Pet, that was rotten and wrong. I don't know what came over me." Pet never, ever let a woman get that close to you again; it can ruin you. I guess I felt I had to help you release yourself from torment, but you're still a virgin. That will give you an idea of how Clay will make you feel if you give yourself to him. And I think you will, the sooner the better, for your sake and mine."

Pet returned to her room at the hotel. She lay upon the bed confused and bewildered, determined that she did love Clay and would see him again.

FIVE

A week had passed. Clay took stock of his position and decided it was time to put his reasons for being in Pueblo into play. He dressed, wearing a white hat, white shirt, stripped pants and the bright yellow vest. Clay came down to breakfast and found Mr. Phillips eating. They greeted each other and began talking. Mr. Phillips told Clay that he was going to Denver to see about buying another bull. Clay liked the idea until Mr. Phillips said, "Keep your eye on Pet while I'm gone. It'll take about ten days."

"All right. But I'm telling you now, if she gets out of hand, I'll not hesitate to spank her hide good." Clay sighed as he stirred in his chair.

Mr. Phillips laughed, but knew Clay meant what he said. Mr. Phillips was pleased that Clay had agreed, and sort of wished Clay would like Pet.

Clay was moved by Pet, so he had his mind set on just how he needed to handle her. He didn't know at the time that Pet also had her mind set on how to handle him.

"Pet will be down soon, Clay. I'm going to ride out to the ranch with her to get a few papers." He looked at his pocket watch.

Clay tossed him a pack of cigarettes saying, "Take a good look at that bull and make sure he's a young one."

"Sure will," replied Mr. Phillips as he opened the pack and took one out.

As Clay and Mr. Phillips were coming from the dining room, Pet came bouncing down the steps.

"Hurry up and let's get going, Pet. Did you eat?"

"No, dad, I'll eat out at the ranch."

"Can't you speak to Clay?"

Pet avoided Clay's eyes and said, "Hi, Clay."

"Morning, Pet."

"What the devil is wrong with you two?" Mr. Phillips demanded as he looked at both these young people.

"Nothing's wrong with me," Pet snapped. "I'm just surprised you consort with woman beaters."

Clay was waiting for this chance to needle her. "Woman beater! What woman did I beat?"

"Me, when you knocked me down."

"Oh, but I thought you were a man."

Then he looked at Mr. Phillips and said, "Hey, Martin, did you ever see a woman dressed like a man and carrying a .38? Hell, I'd say a woman should stay in a woman's place."

"Yeah, I guess you're right, Clay," Mr. Phillips laughed, knowing Clay was deliberately teasing his daughter.

Pet pouted. She glared at her father and threw her golden blond head into the air and stormed out exclaiming, "Damn you, Clay!"

"Real girls wear dresses," Clay called after her.

Mr. Phillips didn't know what to do. Pet was angry

and, knowing her, she wouldn't be quick to forgive him for siding with Clay. He was saved from indecision when Pet's voice sounded through the door, "You coming, Dad?"

Mr. Phillips already had the saddled horses tied to the hotel's hitching rail. As they reached the door Clay said, "You'd better be getting along. That girl of your is sitting on barbed wire in the saddle," his voice carrying to her in the early morning air.

She shouted, "If it was any of your damned business, Clay, I'd show you what I'm sitting on!"

Mr. Phillips blushed at his daughter's remark and quickly mounted. Both rode out of town at a smart canter toward the ranch. As they rode, Pet's mood changed. She questioned her father about Clay. He answered, but didn't tell her Clay was the new marshal. He also realized by her strict questioning that Clay was more of a concern to her than she wanted him or Clay to believe.

"I think he's mean, Dad. And he makes me so nervous."

Mr. Phillips took the remark as a confession of her feelings, and as a way to try to see how he might feel about them.

"Are you trying to say you like Clay?"

"I wish it were as simple as that."

"Pet, I'll tell you. Clay is the man I'd like to see get you. But he won't ask for anything. If you give him the idea that you want him, he'll take you. And, God help the man that would interfere with him and his woman."

"Do you really believe that, dad?"

"Believe it? I know Clay's kind of man, he don't play. And I'm convinced he sure as hell likes you."

Pet was quiet as she listened to her father and thought over everything he said. "Dad, do you really think he cares about me?"

Father and daughter spurred their horses, not stopping until they had arrived at the ranch. After changing clothes, Mr. Phillips called Pet. Seeing her father in his new attire she remarked, "My, you look like a lawyer or something."

"Well, thank you, my dear."

Since it was a hot day the old man was dressed in all white. His heavy stock of white hair contrasted evenly with his clear blue eyes. For a man of fifty-five he was well preserved and took great pride in his fitness. He put his arms around his daughter's shoulders and told her, "Now, I'll be gone for a few days. You stay in town while I'm gone, and for God's sake, Pet, if anything comes up, get to Clay first. He'll be around to sort of look after things for me."

"You mean Clay is to look after me, don't you."

"Well, er – I – well, yes. I feel better when I know he's around. Don't you?"

"In a way, but I won't let the big ape know it," she smiled.

"Well, I've got everything so I'll be seeing you when I return."

Pet kissed her father, and as he left called after him, "Have fun in the big city, but don't you dare get any ideas about finding a stepmother for me."

Her father waved his hand and rode off back to town where he'd catch the train for Denver.

Back in Pueblo, Clay had spent the morning walking around the town. It was Friday and Clay had spent his first week getting to know the layout of the town.

This morning he visited every place of business in town and talked to scores of people. The old banker, Mr. Bryant, was a skeptical and sly man. Clay learned that the biggest ranch in the county belonged to the banker.

While at the bank, Clay opened an account and made a hefty deposit. This helped in getting the banker to talk a bit. Clay learned the assets, the worth of the town and who ran it; the latter of which he already knew. Everywhere he went people refused to discuss Blair Tyson. They only referred to him as the town boss. Clay asked Mr. Bryant why he and some of the other businessmen didn't get together and elect a mayor or sheriff by vote.

"We have, several times, but within three weeks every last one was killed. All accidentally, of course, but everyone knows better."

The banker revealed this information easily, knowing that Clay would learn it soon enough anyway. He was being clever in order to draw any information he could from Clay. Like everyone else in town, the banker was curious to know who he was. Mr. Bryant knew Clay was asking questions for other than civic reasons.

"I suppose, then, Blair moved in?" asked Clay.

"You got the picture, son."

It was clear now that through strong-arm tactics Blair Tyson's men had persuaded the people of Pueblo not to interfere with him, and his word soon became law in the town.

In the general store owned by the Graystones, Pap Graystone was reluctant to talk. But Mr. Graystone, a motherly-looking woman, said, "Young man, people can only stand so much hurt, then they just don't care." She informed Clay that their store had been out for lease. Blair Tyson, with two of his men, always came to see the new owners of businesses, showing them an old land grant with a lot of legal looking papers declaring him to be the heir of a grandfather who had done the government a long and good service for which the government had rewarded him with some large parcels of land, and, upon examination of a map, it showed that all of Pueblo and over half of the county was owned by Blair.

Mr. Graystone joined his wife and told Clay that they had sent to Washington to verify this and that a letter had come back stating it was true. Mr. Graystone then said, "So if we stay on his land, he charges us. Now, mind you, every one of us has to pay him a tax – a land tax of a hundred dollars a year, to be paid quarterly. If we can't meet the tax, he'll give you five hundred dollars for your business and pay you half of the profits to run it."

Clay, after learning all this, asked, "What about the bank?"

"Old Bryant declares it's legal, and Tyson is a lawyer, you know. And, I heard he also holds one fourth interest in the bank."

Mrs. Graystone added, "Blair always jokes that if the bank were to go broke, he would stand the loss out of his interest alone."

"I guess he could," said Clay, now wondering why Mr. Bryant hadn't told him of Blair's interest in the bank.

After buying a few things, Clay left the store. After all he had learned, he realized that Tyson and his men had full control of the town. He also wondered why Mr. Phillips had never mentioned this to him, and again wondered why the banker had said nothing about Blair owning one fourth of the bank. The rest of the stores and small shops declared they were doing a steady business because the town was growing and a lot of people were settling in and around Pueblo. They couldn't complain too much about the tax because they were still making money.

"But not what they should be making," thought Clay.

Clay was actually surprised at the vise Blair Tyson had, and the land Blair claimed to own kept coming into his mind. With a hold on this office, he thought Blair could just about claim any section of land he wished, especially if it proved profitable, like the Phillips dairy ranch.

Clay became aware of a key piece that was just fitting into place to this puzzle in Pueblo. He made a rapid decision, and instead of returning to the hotel he went to the railroad station. He talked to the telegraph operator for a few seconds and give him the following message to send off immediately:

Major Mart I, Campton
Austin, Texas, Dept.-25
Dear Uncle Mart,

Please send more cigarettes. Check and send information on all land grants issued by government within the last fifteen years. Forward all mail to: Phillips Hotel, Pueblo, Colorado.

Repeat: Check land grants from Washington. Would have to be issued through capital at Austin for this southwestern district.

Your nephew,
Clay

The telegrapher looked at the message and then back at Clay. "That will be two dollars."

Clay handed him the money. Still the man looked inquisitive. "Mind if I ask what the word 'cigarettes' is?" he inquired.

Clay laughed and withdrew a pack and gave it to the operator, saying, "Ready-rolled ones."

"You don't say! I've heard of these things, but didn't believe it. I'll get the message right off, mister. And thanks."

SIX

On his way back to the hotel, Clay stopped at the livery stable to ask the man to exercise his horse, Baldy, giving him a dollar for the trouble. Discovering that he was hungry, Clay went straight to the hotel to cure his desire.

The waitress took his order, and when she returned with the food she leaned close and bent over, giving Clay a good look down the front of her bosom. He smiled in appreciation of the view, but his mind went directly to Pet. He thought of her as he ate, and grew into a physical picture of satisfaction with his feeling of wanting her. He was beginning to feel the fire in his loins and knew the only relief he wanted was Pet. It made him angry when he thought of her supple, wide hips extending from such a boyish waist. The thought of her wearing a gun and blue jeans displeased him, yet he figured she just didn't know the full potential of her body. He wondered if she thought in a woman's terms, especially where he was concerned.

He finished his meal, still thinking of Pet. When he got up from the table, the waitress was watching him and saw the heavy, telltale outlines of his excitement.

There was no doubt in her mind that she'd caused Clay's situation.

Since no one else was in the room, she boldly walked over to Clay and said, "God, fellow, what are you going to do with that? Can I have it?"

Clay looked at her in surprise, not actually knowing what she meant. She then stood close and felt him through his pants. He felt a surge of heat and bashfulness as she said softly, "Sure is nice, come on upstairs and give it to me."

Clay was flustered; he didn't how to get out of the awkward moment. He stood there, as she pressed hard into him and whispered, "Come on. It won't cost you nothing. Come on upstairs, I'll be waiting."

The waitress raced up the stairs, tugging at the bottom of her dress. Clay wanted to follow, although what he wanted most was Pet. His desires overwhelmed him and up the steps he went. The waitress was eagerly looking for him and called softly, "Down here."

When he closed the door she was out of her dress, lying on the bed in a white slip pulled up over her middle. His first gaze was at her pink thighs.

"Come on!" she coaxed in an excited whisper.

He went to her and she reached out and seized him firmly. After a five-minute lapse of time she whispered, "Man, you're good, so good. Will you give it to me some more?"

Clay never answered her question but listened as the girl breathed, "It's damn good to have a man on top of me after that bastard Texas Red."

Having both dressed, they sat on the side of the bed smoking.

"Is Texas Red your man?"

"Yeah. And he'd kill us both if he knew about this. But he can't satisfy me. Besides, I get tired of letting him peep at me. He likes it that way. He says it's better to watch than actually do it sometimes."

"What do you think?" asked Clay.

"Hell, mister, I like to lay on my back and actually do it, unless a man really wants to give it to me like some fellows have."

"How's that?"

"A woman's God-damned delightful lip service. God, that's good. You want me to – no, I guess you wouldn't. You don't know about that business. You would knock my head off if I wanted to do it to you that way, wouldn't you?"

"Every man to his own. I'll take mine the old conventional way." Clay reached in his pocket and handed her some money.

"No thanks. What God gave me - I give you. I don't sell it. I like it too much." When Clay laughed she asked, "Again some time, huh?"

"Maybe, but you're Red's woman."

"Oh, I see. Everybody's scared of Red except me. I can make him do anything I want him to. And I mean, anything! Guess I'll see you around, mister. You better leave before I want some more."

Clay left relieved but disgusted with himself for being such a pushover in a moment of weakness. He felt only pity and a deep sadness for the waitress. His only enjoyment was to think in his mind that the woman he'd just had was Pet. He learned of Texas Red's nature and figured that pinpointed him as the peeping Tom of Pueblo. He still thought about Pet, and said to himself, "Damn you, Pet, why do you torture me this way?"

Clay left his room after shaving and changing pants. He again put cigarettes in his pocket, looked at his guns and smiled. "Soon," he almost said aloud.

He failed to see the men going into the jail building, but they saw him as he passed. Billy Ferrell, who had gone to Leadville after shooting the Phillips bull, had returned a few days earlier with Hank, the man Blair had sent for. They watched Clay enter the Payday Casino. Blair said, "All right, Billy, you want to have some fun with that yellow-vested stranger... we'll do it tonight."

Texas Red roared with laughter and held up a pair of women's long-legged bloomers. "Hey Billy, we're going to see how he looks in these fancy pants."

"I'll put 'em on him, too," smiled Billy.

Blair produced a bottle of whiskey and passed it around. He looked at each of his men gathered here. There was Mex, an evil looking fat-faced Mexican who was feared as a knife wielder; complete with a ten-inch blade he carried in his belt. He was a sneaky killer. Even Texas Red, the cold-blooded, right-handed killer for Blair, didn't crowd Mex. Hank, a big brute of a man was also there, who, with his bull-like strength, could break a man in two with his bare hands and had proven it for fun. There was also a mean half-breed whose pleasure it was to carve out a living man's heart. With Texas Red riding herd on this crew, they'd become the terror of the four surrounding states. No lawman ever stayed or worked in Pueblo or its county. The other men were just hired guns that would kill. They were easily led. Blair never let any of these men too far in on his plans.

"All right, Blair, let's get down to cases," said Texas

Red. He continued, "We've got a little job of our own to do."

Blair walked over to the desk and laid out a sheet of paper with a map drawn on it. "This is the plan." He began to explain, pointing to each man's part as he was talking. "To begin with, the railroad company and the mint think they're doing a slick job, but I've got the dope. There will be over two hundred fifty thousand dollars in paper money and minted gold heavily guarded by federal men and army troopers."

"So what do we do?" chimed up Billy.

"Billy, we do nothing. It's a fake shipment to pull anybody who's interested off the track. The real shipment of money will be on the 4:30 local going into Kansas City. That train leaves Pueblo around 2:15 on July first. That gives us about three weeks.

"Boy, that's a real good set up," said Texas Red.

"Where will the money be?" Mex wanted to know.

"That's a good question. The money won't be in the safe of the baggage car but in the caboose where the train men ride."

"How many guards?" asked one of the men.

"Two," answered Blair.

"No way in hell for us to miss that," said Texas Red.

Blair again looked at the men around him and spoke, "Now, this is the way we'll do it. Pete, you and Snyder be at Bells Crossing with five horses. Joe and Weaver will be here at Hills Rest with the other five mounts. These will be our changing points. Leave in time so the horses won't be winded, it's a long ride back here to Pueblo. Here's something else. As soon as we change horses, take the tired mounts back to the shack and shoot them. Burn the saddles and the shack, then come on into Pueblo."

"Christ, for that kind of money I'd burn my own Ma," echoed the Half-Breed.

Every man in the room looked at him, knowing that he meant what he'd said.

"What about the rest of us?" Hank wanted to know.

"Hank, you and Billy be in Denver and on the train when it pulls out. When the train gets past the mouth of Posto Canyon, Billy, you walk outside. Hank, you go inside and cover anyone who's in the caboose. Billy, when you hear Hank give you the okay, you uncouple the caboose from the train and then turn the brake wheel till it stops. The rest of us will see you, and a log will be thrown across the tracks to help stop the caboose. I don't have to tell you, this will be our last job. So, if you have to shoot, make it count. The rest of you, Texas, Mex and the Half-Breed, will be with me to help get the caboose stopped. Now is everything clear to everybody?"

No one asked any questions. They all agreed it was smooth plan.

Blair sized up each of the men, then said, in a cold sounding voice, "Now everyone listen to this. After you've had your fun with that stranger tonight, I don't want any bullshit from any of you until this job is pulled off. Then you can shoot the hell out of each other if you want to. And, as I said before, with your share of the money and mine, I'm going to buy the governorship of this damned state and you all can come along. Agreed?"

"Hell yes!" they shouted.

"I can see Texas Red Morgan now, 'Ye Honorable Marshal of the state.'" The entire crew, including Blair, laughed at Hank's remark.

"Texas Red Morgan stood up and yawned, saying, "Is that all, Blair? Let's go take care of that fancy vest. After tonight he'll be known as the bloomer boy." Again he fluttered and waved the pair of long-legged bloomers in the air, causing the men to roar with laughter. Afterwards, they made a few comments and headed out to the Payday Casino to find Clay, the man with the yellow vest.

In the Payday Casino Clay was having a drink and talking to Kate. The place was always full of men and a few women besides the girls that worked for Kate.

Kate kept tabs on the girls and on the men by having an extra bouncer around, just in case some men felt once wasn't enough for the five dollars. They all came in – miners, cowpokes and others. The place had taken on a smell of sweat and bay rum mixed with raw whiskey and heavy beer. The gambling tables were in full session. One thing could be said of the Payday: Kate did run honest and straight games at her place. Word was, "Kate is straight," which meant lady luck fans came to her place to find a square deal.

Kate was standing behind the bar talking to Clay. They were having quite a few laughs over Kate's last remark, "Clay, this ol' girl's played out…"

Kate felt like talking. She poured another drink for them and said with a sigh, "You know, Clay, if you were a real handsome man I'd understand women, even myself, falling for you." Kate was thinking mostly of Pet – "but," she continued, "with your looks and that rugged way you walk and talk to women makes them almost pee on themselves."

"Kate, cut it out. You told me that years ago."

"Sure did, and it still holds true." Tell me, Clay, you don't have to, but I'm just wondering, how do you feel about..."

"Pet? That's what you want to know isn't it?" Clay cut in.

"Well, yes, it is."

"All right, I'll tell you. I'm crazy as hell about her. But that little heifer makes my ass tired, wearing that damned gun and those god-forsaken jeans of hers."

"God knows you're the man for her, and the only one who can dominate her. That's what she needs." Kate caught her breath and laid her hand on Clay's arm with almost an embrace. "Clay, I shouldn't tell you this, but that girl loves the hell out of you. And as you might guess, she's a piece of untouched fruit. Take her. Not too gently, but you take her and make it just as soon as possible. That's my advice. Take it from a woman who knows and understands women."

Clay felt the physical sensation creeping again, and was thankful the bar hid him. He wanted to say something else to Kate but she had moved away. He slowly turned from the bar in the smoke-filled air just in time to see some men pushing their way through the crowd towards him. He felt a tinge of regret for not having his guns. He started away from the bar and recognized Blair Tyson with a grin on his face and Texas Red Morgan with a pair of pink cotton bloomers swinging in his hands. He also saw Billy Ferrell, and recalled the events that had taken place when they'd last met; the first man he'd had trouble with in Pueblo and in the same place.

SEVEN

As the nine men crowded toward Clay, Kate jerked her head up. She knew this meant trouble. She dashed behind the bar where the bartender kept a sawed-off shotgun. Clay moved back against the bar.

"Hey, there!" shouted Billy Ferrell. At the sound of his thundering voice, men stopped what they were doing to see what was going on. The girls released the clutch they had on prospective customers and gathered around each other in a bunch.

"Is your name Clay?" Billy asked. The saloon went deathly still.

"That's right," answered Clay coldly. "I told you I didn't mean any harm the other day."

"Did you now, yellow vest?"

The muscles in Clay's body tensed to steel as he replied, "I'd do it again if I had the chance."

"All right, mister. Since you want to be so uppity about it, with your ass on your nose, I wonder if you'd mind dressing in these fancy pants to go with that pretty yellow vest." Billy took the pink bloomers from Texas Red.

"Go plumb to hell, fella."

This whole scheme was to humiliate Clay, to teach him a lesson in front of everyone.

Blair spoke. "Now, if the gentleman will just apologize to Billy, that would be appreciated."

"What I said once, I say again. Bring that damned horse in here again, Billy, and I'll kill you!"

A gasp went up from the crowd, not realizing that Clay meant what he'd just said.

"That will be enough, Blair. Get your men out of here," demanded Kate.

"Listen, Kate, when a guy gets out of line with one of my men, it's tough. Unless he makes it easy on himself, like setting up the house, which is good for your business, or he apologizes. But this stranger went too far. Hell, every saddle punk coming through town might think we're soft. So, Kate, you stay the hell out of this or else."

"He's not a stranger. I know him."

Blair walked over to Kate. "You should pick better friends," he said. With an open hand he slapped Kate a stinging blow across the face.

"Don't nobody breathe!" demanded Texas Red with a lightning fast draw. His gun hand was itching to throw lead at anyone, in any direction.

Pushing his way through the crowd and walking to the front, the Half-Breed said with a loud shout, "Hell, Billy, either make the bastard put them bloomers on and walk out or let us put them on him and carry him out."

The men in the gang laughed and Billy said, "What'll it be, mister?"

Clay saw that he had no choice but to fight like hell; the devil take whatever left. Instead of waiting on them to come for him, he placed one foot back against the bar for a spring. He knew Kate couldn't help him and neither could the bartender. In fact, he knew the situation was more than the entire crowd could deal with.

He withdrew his pack of cigarettes to distract them. He calmly lit one and puffed long and hard to get a fire on the tip. Then suddenly Clay pushed with his foot and sprang toward Texas Red with swinging fists like maulers crashing into human flesh. He fought a good fight for a few seconds. Even though he knocked Texas Red down, the full fury of the gang fell upon him like a pack of lions on a zebra. They used their fists like clubs, beating Clay down to the floor. He staggered as he was falling, helped down with a kick and a neatly laid gun barrel alongside his head.

When he laid still the men, led by Hank, held Clay while Billy drew the pink bloomers up over his legs until they fit. The all laughed. Even the crowd laughed. Blair Tyson poured a bottle of whiskey all over the humiliated Clay, saying, "Looks like fancy pants pissed on himself."

The place was bedlam. Kate managed to stop crying and looked upon Clay lying sprawled on the floor in the wet, soggy female garments. She couldn't laugh at him and felt a haunting pity for those who did.

"Laugh now," she said, "because when he comes for you you'll all be on your way to hell. Now get out of here, you've had your fun."

She started to where Clay lay but was pushed back by Texas Red. "He doesn't need your help, Kate. We're going and we'll take him with us."

"Bring him along," cried Billy, nursing his blistered cheek.

Three of the men dragged Clay's body outside where they tied a rope around his feet and threw the other end around Billy's saddle horn.

Blair ordered, "Now, Billy, slowly drag him up to the end of the street. That ought to fix him up real nice."

Kate, along with all the girls from the Payday, emptied out of the place to see what else they would do to Clay.

"It's a damned shame," said one of the girls.

"Not one bastard will help him," sighed another.

Kate tried to push forward, but Texas Red grabbed her wrists and held her tightly in front of him. As she struggled, he could feel the full curves of her rump against him. He undulated once or twice behind her. Just as Kate felt his hardness he quickly jerked a couple of times and spent himself.

Kate knew from the jerking what had happened. She turned herself around to face him and growled, "You queer son of a bitch. Your mother must have been a dog." Then she drew in her cheeks and spit squarely in his face.

Blair, seeing Kate's fury, knew Red was fixing to raise hell at Kate. He checked him.

"I should kill you," said Kate, walking back to her saloon.

"Little bitch," muttered Red, wiping the spit from his face.

"Damn Red, it looked like you were getting a piece," said Mex. Texas Red glanced at Mex as Blair watched both of them.

Pet Phillips had just ridden in from the ranch. She was rounding the corner by the livery stable when she saw the sidewalks jammed with people and heard men shouting "Look at fancy pants! Hey, take them off, fancy vest."

The loud noise of laughter and a few squeals from the half drunk women penetrated Pet's ears. She pulled her horse up short when a tall horseman, about the age of twenty-five, stopped his horse a few feet in front of her and looked back. The man's face was hard, and from the light of the moon and the buildings she saw his hate-filled eyes. What upset her the most was that she recognized the rider as a Negro.

She exclaimed almost aloud, "A nigger rider!"

Pet had seen many Negroes, but this particular one had startled her into uneasiness, something between fear and disbelief. She could see the Negro had a light brown complexion. She prompted her little mare forward and passed the man, feeling his eyes upon her every move. The Negro even moved his horse in the same direction down the street.

Because of the noise, Pet slid from her horse in front of the hotel to see what the cause for all the excited shouting might be. She pushed her way through the crowd and stood transfixed as she saw Clay, bloody and dirty, wearing wet bloomers cracked with mud, being dragged slowly up the street.

She raised her hands to her face as if to blot out the sight, and cried, "Oh, no!"

She ran to Billy Ferrell's side, pleading for him to stop. But he didn't stop, he only laughed harder. She whirled away directly into Texas Red who grabbed her. One of the other men of the gang, seeing Red holding her, yelled out, "That's about as close as you'll ever get to that piece of pussy, Tex, better feel her good."

Pet broke from Texas Red's grasp and ran up the

street yelling and begging as she ran. "For God's sake, somebody stop them! Please, somebody help!" She only got stares from the men who looked on.

She made a lunge for her .38 but Texas Red, who had been following her, knocked it right out of her hand. She screamed as she kicked back high into his middle.

"Hey, Red, that little bitch will ruin you, boy," Hank called out.

Pet broke away again and ran. She was almost out of breath from shock, fear and desperation. The effort she was making was to no avail. She looked at the sea of blank faces and her head began to spin. She stumbled back into the side of the Negro's horse.

The Negro sat tall in his saddle, watching the crowd draw within ten feet of him.

"Won't somebody do something, please?" Pet cried again.

She was about to faint when the Negro asked, "Is that your man, Miss?"

Pet couldn't believe her ears. "What can a nigger do?" she thought. Responding as if he were a log floating to a drowning victim in a raging river she cried out, "Yes! Oh, yes."

The crowd had become aware of the Negro on the blue roan horse. Some had even overheard him ask Pet if Clay was her man.

Billy stopped his horse. Texas Red Morgan held up his hand, drawing the other men back. Even Blair stood in cold agitation.

The tall Negro spoke again to Pet. "Where do you want him, Miss?"

"Over there in the hotel," she managed to answer.

The Negro stepped out of his saddle. He stood a good six feet two, weighing about two hundred twenty pounds.

Kate had again ventured out of the Payday. She saw the big Negro wearing a black Stetson, light blue shirt and blue striped pants tucked into a pair of expensive black boots. He had two .44s with cherry handles tied down very low. His stride was long and easy and his slimness from the waist down was perfect, setting off his monstrously wide shoulders.

Without hesitation, he took a thin blade knife from his belt and, in a calculating gesture, cut the rope holding Clay from Billy Ferrell's saddle horn. Without even looking at the crowd, he picked up Clay's dragged body in his massive strong arms.

"Jesus, look at the graceful movements of that black!" exclaimed Kate in awe. She was as taken in by his actions as the others.

"Well, I'll be damned," said another one of the girls.

"Now that nigger's either loco or he's flirting with hell," sighed Texas Red.

The Negro's boldness and fearlessness caused even the hard killers to respect him; even causing them to wonder if he was one of their kind. No one would move to hinder the black man as Pet led him to the hotel.

The crowd wouldn't move on. The just milled around outside the hotel waiting for what, they weren't sure. Blair's men moved over to him with questions on their faces. Finally Blair issued an order in a whisper, "The nigger is fair game, after the job, for a thousand dollars."

"Listen, Blair, we can't let a nigger just ride into town and get away with that. Hell, he made us a laughing stock."

"That's right," the rest of the gang chimed in.

"All right, Snyder, you and Pete take care of him when he comes out. Is that fair enough, boys?"

"Yeah," said Texas Red, "and I'm betting fifty on Snyder. Any takers?"

"Here's mine. I think Pete will get 'em."

They made bets all around as they crossed over to the side of the general store to wait.

Inside the hotel Pet had the colored man place Clay on his bed. The Negro took out his knife again and cut the whiskey drenched offensive bloomers from his body.

"Get him some water, Miss. I'll undress him."

Pet hadn't been gone a good ten minutes when the man had Clay undressed and under the covers. With the hot water she'd brought back, they washed the bruises and cleaned the matted blood from Clay's body. Pet was pleased to discover he had no real serious wounds; only persistent and miserable sand cuts.

EIGHT

The Negro held Clay up and forced some whiskey down his throat. Clay coughed two or three times and began to return to the land of the living. His eyes opened first upon Pet, and he asked, "What the hell happened?" He felt his body and tried to rise up.

"Better lay still for a spell," said the Negro.

Clay looked to where the voice had come from and saw the tall, brawny man for the first time.

"What the hell is this? Do I know you, Mister?"

For the first time Pet saw the broad, friendly smile on the strange black man's face. She felt warmness as he replied, "That doesn't really matter now, does it? How do you feel?"

"Like hell and then some."

Pet, feeling much better herself, answered, "It's no wonder. They might have killed you. If it hadn't been for this man, riding in from out of nowhere and daring to ask me if you were my man when no one else would help, I think they would have."

Clay started to say something and then saw the pink bloomers hanging over the back of the chair. Pet had to laugh a bit.

"I remember now. They must have slow-dragged me, too."

"They did," said the Negro, laughing a little.

Clay didn't become angry, as Pet had thought he would. Instead, he laughed the laugh of a dead man. "Hand me those fancy pants. Last thing I remember, they were trying to put them on me. I guess they managed it."

"They did," said Pet, as she handed him the ragged apparel.

He looked at them and conceived a plot in the back of his mind. "I'll keep these for a while. Now, tell me what all happened... and what do we call our new friend, fella?"

The Negro stood to his full height. Pet looked up at him as he replied, "My name is Diamond Clifford. My friends call me Cliff. I guess your woman can tell you the full story. I'll be on my way since it looks like you'll be all right."

"Wait, Cliff," said Pet.

She stood over Clay telling him all she knew and how Diamond had helped him when no one else would.

Clay, thinking clearly despite his mammoth headache, said, "Cliff, you can't go out there; they're still waiting for you. Listen."

Cliff looked at Clay and Pet. "Well, I sure can't stay here!"

"Who says you can't stay. My father owns this hotel."

"That's not what I mean, Miss."

"Call me Pet, or Ellen."

"What I mean, Pet, is that I came in here and I've gotta go back out there. A man's got to do what he's got to do. You understand, don't you, Clay?"

"I guess I do more than anybody else. I'll go with you, Diamond."

Pet sat on the bed quickly as he started to get up. "Clay, you aren't up to it. I'll give Diamond a place to stay. What do you say?"

"I just couldn't do that, Pet. I'll cause you too much trouble."

"No more than you've already caused just by helping me and Pet," commented Clay.

The three newly bound friends were interrupted by a voice shouting, "Hey, black boy, you've got to come out sometime... and we'll be waiting."

Diamond smiled hard. "I guess they mean me."

Clay laughed. "You might be black, but I don't figure you're even scared of the devil himself."

Diamond appreciated Clay's remark and shot right back, "Didn't you know, he's my cousin?"

"Kissing or once-removed?" asked Pet, enjoying the laugh with the men.

Clay's eyes fell upon the two guns tied low on Diamond. "You'll do all right."

Diamond loosened both guns with a slight movement of his arms. "Miss – I mean, Pet – if it's all right with you, I'll stay here tonight after I put my horse away." Then he left the room without another word.

Pet looked frightened.

"He'll be back," Clay assured her. "Blow out the light, Pet, and hand me those pants over there."

She gave him the pants and blew out the light. Clay jumped into them and went to the dresser drawer and removed his guns.

"Come on!" he whispered to Pet.

Pet followed him down the steps to the front door.

They saw Diamond walking from the porch steps.

"There he is, Snyder! Pete!" Texas Red called.

Both gunmen came forward. A voice from the gang hollered, "Draw, black boy, and tell the devil hello!"

Diamond walked slowly towards the two men. He was taking their hearts by his slow stealth. Their hands flashed to their guns. Those watching only saw the Negro bend slightly backward. As he reached as if to sit, it appeared as if his large hands paused or hesitated over the cherry butts of his .44s. They saw nothing more, but heard two shots then saw two men pitch forward, looking like billy goats, glassy-eyed in death. As the men fell, their guns fired into the ground from reflex action.

"Jesus Christ, they had their guns out way before he did!" said Texas Red.

"God Almighty!" said Blair.

Diamond re-holstered the murderous weapons, letting the click of their hammers sound an echo of more if others wished to try him. He then asked aloud, "I'd call it a fair fight, wouldn't you men?"

"Hell, yes," said the Half-Breed.

The rest of the gang turned to stare at the Half-Breed for running his mouth. Blair and Texas Red stepped forward. Diamond was still ready to go for his guns if the need arose.

"No more gun play, fellow. Look me up when you get settled. I'm Blair Tyson; this here is Texas Red Morgan. Maybe I can find a job for you."

Texas Red recoiled, but respected the tall Negro's handiwork with guns.

"Name's Diamond - I'll listen, Tyson. It never hurts a man to listen. And that proves it," Diamond said pointing to the last two departed men, "by way of hell."

"Let's go, boys. We'll see you around, Diamond." Blair moved off with his men lapping at his heels.

Pet and Clay waited until Diamond had returned from stabling his horse. Pet gave him a room down the hall. They said good night, watching the tall Negro go into his room.

"It's really late," Pet said as she ushered Clay upstairs. "And just look at you. Go on up and I'll bring you some pie and coffee."

Clay waited in his room feeling refreshed after he washed his face. Pet came in carrying a tray laden with coffee and pie. She cut a slice and poured a cup of coffee for her man.

"What did you tell him? When he asked if I were your man, I mean."

"I said yes. What else could I saw if I wanted his help?"

"Woman in distress, huh. Did you mean what you said?"

Pet looked at him, shirtless and still barefoot. "At the time I did."

"Oh," said Clay, a bit disappointed.

"Good night, Clay." Pet gathered up the tray and rushed out of the room.

Within an hour she had returned to Clay's room. She rapped on the door softly.

"Come on in, it's open."

Like a pixie she sneaked in, closing the door and locking it. The glow from the moon gave enough light, but Pet drew the shade and lit the lamp. She sat on the side of the bed and looked at Clay, who was already in bed, and said, "I couldn't go to bed like this."

"Like how?"

"You know!"

"Pet, what's wrong with you?"

She turned facing him and saw where the sheet was being held up by his need. She laughed a little at the sight and said, "I meant what I told Diamond."

"You did?"

"Yeah. You know I did. And I was thinking back in my room that a good man, after a good fight, needs to have his woman give him a good piece."

Clay raced out of the bed and took her hand. She snatched the only sheet covering him and said, "Let me look at you, Clay. I want to see all of you." She saw him and wanted all that she saw. She patted him and said, "I want the man I love to look at me and see me, too."

She removed her blouse and jeans, standing naked before him. She lingered there for a short time, then moved closer to the bed. "Look at me, Clay. Feel me. I want to see the desire in your eyes. I want my man to know every inch of me."

Clay looked and ran his hand over her pink flesh. She became a flame of heat and passion.

"That's it, Clay, that's what I want. Don't be ashamed of my body, I'm not ashamed of yours."

"Clay, teach me how to love you. Tell me that you want me. I'll give you anything I've got."

Clay felt strangeness from this woman. She was so young, so pure; yet he'd have to hurt her to start her love flowing.

"Clay, I'm no woman until I've had all of you. God, Clay, make me your woman!"

She crawled under him, breathing impatiently.

It was fascinating to watch her. Clay whispered, "Pet, this may hurt a little bit."

"I expect it will, but I want it Clay."

He thenmade love to her.

Afterward, Pet lay with a smile on her face, now that her body had found the peace it had sought and longed for. Clay dozed off to sleep, tired but happy to have fulfilled what was desired of him only to be awakened by her.

"Come on, wake up." She had a basin of water and cleaned him with tenderness and kissed the cause of her new found happiness.

Clay blushed, "Does it mean that much to you?"

She still held him, looking. "Did I do enough? I want to do more. What else can I do, Clay?"

He was moved to tears himself, saying, "Pet, you've done the best. You've given me all of you; I could ask for nothing more."

She believed him and knew he meant what he said. He was her man forever and she was his woman.

NINE

To understand the people of Pueblo, you had to understand that the town was a wide-open place without law or order. Blair Tyson, as the voice of everything, had spread a maze of fear over the people. Whatever happened, as long as it didn't concern them personally, was of no interest. They had no incentive, save that of survival. Yet, when the news of a Negro killing two white men got around, their complacency was shattered, but not to the extent of retaliation. They waited to hear what Blair Tyson would say and do. After all, it was his men who were killed. Still, underneath the surface, they felt their backs straightening out a little bit. At least one man, and a black man, had stood up to the gang and lived to tell about it. This is what they all talked about in hushed tones among friends. The whole truth of the matter was that the shooting had begun a stirring amid the people. What direction the new feelings of the town would take would be left upon the shoulders of one man – Clay Clinton – who was now coming from the Phillips Hotel wearing a bright yellow vest and a pair of ivory-handled guns, tied low. High on the left side of his vest was a bright shinning star, for all to see, that read, "U.S. Marshal."

Pet stood on the porch of the hotel, thrilled beyond words at the sight of the man she loved. His working clothes were all black, except for the vest. She marveled and experienced a deeper respect and a feeling of worship for Clay as she saw him now. She couldn't really believe that the man she'd fallen in love with was indeed a lawman.

Meanwhile, on the front street up on the second floor of the bank, a meeting was being held to determine if this black man was an asset or a liability. Without Diamond knowing as he and Blair Tyson talked, the banker was listening to the whole conversation. Although Blair had singled out the need for the black man, the banker still had no particular use for him.

Diamond, considering the chat he'd had with Blair, decided it was time to talk with Clay concerning his aspects and expectations, knowing that no matter what Clay thought, he had a job to do – like it or not.

Down on the street again, Diamond's eyes watched Pet as she stood on the hotel porch. He also saw Clay and made his way towards him. When they met, there was almost a terse smile on Diamond's lips, which quickly turned into a broad grin. Then, and only then, did the slight tension in Clay relax into a small warmth, remembering how this black man had handled himself upon their first meeting.

As they talked, discussing the meeting with Blair, Diamond revealed that he was to give Blair some answers and Clay understood just what that meant and its implications. Diamond told Clay how Blair, Texas Red Morgan and Mex had reacted to him regarding the two dead gang members. Clay looked at Diamond and searched deeply to find a bit of remorse but there was none. Again he felt relieved.

"God," he thought, "what a cold bastard!"

Pet finally left the hotel porch and both Clay and Diamond noticed and thought it would be a good time to end their toe-drawing-in-the-dirt conversation. Realizing from all indications what the situation was getting to be, Clay asked without hesitation, "Do you know what Blair wants, Cliff?"

"Sure. It's plain to see."

"And are you going to hire out to him?" Clay asked, deadly serious.

"I'm not a killer."

"But what you might not realize is, if you refuse to join them they'll see fit to remember that you killed two white men. They'll put pressure on me to arrest you, if they don't hang you first. They'll be out to get you, and me."

Diamond's face became a tight smile as he said, "Whether we like it or not, we've got each other."

This was the bare truth as things stood. Clay realized he would need help, and there was no other man he could depend upon but this Negro. He had confidence in Diamond, but the man's dislike for the law could be a problem.

"Cliff, you black son of a bitch, you have caused me a lot of trouble."

"Clay, you white son of a bitch, so far your life and mine depend on each other."

Clay smiled after calling Diamond the name and Diamond laughed hard at Clay's good nature.

"I'm curious, Clay. What are you going to do about last night?"

"I'm going to make Blair and Billy eat them drawers."

"Now that I gotta see. Since this is a personal thing, the law won't have a hand, will it?"

"No."

"Then you've got a right arm."

Clay appreciated the gesture. Now he was sure of his black friend, knowing their guns were together. He punched Diamond and said, "You figure out a way, don't you, Diamond."

Diamond laughed.

Clay became pensive. "Cliff, I've got a question I've just got to ask. I'd have to do it sooner or later, anyway. A man comes to a hellhole like this for one of three reasons. Either he's running away from something or someone, hiding from something or someone or looking for something or someone – usually to kill. Does one of them fit you?"

"Yeah, I guess one of them fits me; I'll tell you which one when I see the man."

That was enough for Clay. He had the man's word, which to him was as good as his own guns; they were deadly true.

He asked, "You going to be hanging around town here? Or do you want a job?"

"I'll stick around out of your way for a day or so, then find a job. I haven't forgotten I want to see a couple of men eat a pair of drawers."

They both laughed at the prospect of this. Clay and his new friend talked for almost an hour or more before the town had become fully awake. People passing them, seeing Clay with the heavy guns strapped on his narrow waist and the gleaming badge pinned to his vest, began to feel a sense of pride, appreciation and respect for the fancy-vested stranger who had come into their lives.

U.S. Marshal Clay Clinton made his presence known all over the town of Pueblo. He could see the surprise and gratefulness of each shop owner as he visited them all. They began to talk freely, feeling confidence in the man. If he asked anything of them, they gave it, without stopping to ask why.

Mr. Graystone had declared that the town would become a Mecca for peace loving people. All Mrs. Graystone could say from her heartfelt surprise was, "Thanks be to God, a real lawman at last."

The banker, Mr. Bryant, was the only one not too well pleased. Clay noted it and, remembering what he'd learned from the Graystones, easily reasoned why. In some way he was connected to Blair Tyson.

When Clay went into Madam LaCall's shop, she exclaimed with joy, speaking something in French that he didn't understand, but deemed as good.

All along the street men and women almost stopped to gape. Younger women began to see him as a protector of their virtue. Older women beamed proudly, seeing him as the son they could be proud of. The men's respect for the marshal seemed to make them find new courage. The old holster at the livery stable had slapped his thigh at the sight of Clay and said, "By God, son, if I can do anything to help, let me know!" The change in the atmosphere of the town filled Clay with courage.

At lunch the waitress had almost run to him to take his order and then stood around dreamy eyed. The few men that were also eating in the dining room had all greeted him kindly. "Hi, Marshal."

"Nice to see you, Marshal."

"Hello, Marshal."

The news traveled faster than a wind-whipped brush fire in dry season. Only now it had personal bearing on the people of the town. When Clay walked into the Payday, Kate had already heard the news. But when she saw the star on his vest for herself, she echoed in a loud voice, "Clay, I knew it! I told you I always thought you were a lawman."

Clay smiled modestly. A few gamblers and fellows who had seen Blair and his men throw Clay a little party the night before, remarked, "There'll be hell to pay now."

"Yeah," said another one of the Payday patrons. "I think I'd better start spending some time with my old woman at night. Things around here won't be so healthy, especially for Tyson!"

As Clay passed one of the tables where the girls always sat, one chimed, "Marshal, don't forget we're only working girls."

"You know what?" another said, "Free."

Kate laughed, and so did Clay. Clay bought a drink for the girls, Kate and himself. No one mentioned the previous night's events but they all knew it would be settled in a most unforgettable way.

Meanwhile, since Diamond had last talked to Clay, he'd been to see Blair Tyson again, with Billy Ferrell and Texas Red Morgan sitting in on the interview. The rest of the men were over at the jail. Blair was worked up from the news about Clay, yet he nor any of his men had seen him for themselves.

The first thing he had asked when Diamond arrived was, "Is it true, is Clay a U.S. Marshal?"

"Stars, guns and all," replied Cliff.

Texas Red, looking sour, said, "Let's get down to the meat of the subject."

"You in a hurry, fellow?" Diamond asked.

"Hell, no, I just want to get some fresh air!"

"Go on out, Red. I'll tell you the results," said Blair.

Texas Red cast a suspicious look at Billy and remarked, "I'll wait."

Blair took over. "You got any idea why I wanted to talk to you, boy?"

"The name's Diamond. Don't forget it... Yeah, I've got an idea."

"Let's hear it," said Blair.

"No, you seem to be running things around here as well as anybody, so I'd rather the boss talked. That way there's no misunderstandings."

Blair swelled out his chest, thinking the Negro had paid him a compliment, and remarked, "You got good eyes, anyhow, Diamond. How would you like to hire out and work for me? After all, you did away with two of my best men, and they need to be replaced. If you work for me you won't have any worries from the law, or from my boys, for what you did last night."

The big brown Negro almost laughed in Blair's face as he recalled Clay's words from earlier. "I've got to have time to think," he said.

Texas Red snarled, "It didn't take you no time to think last night!"

"No, it didn't, but this is bigger and much more important, I suspect. Just what would my job be?"

"Well, now, that depends on what's to be done," cut in Billy quickly.

"And who would I take orders from? What's the pay? And do I work alone or with another man?"

"Now I can't really answer that last question now, but your pay would be good, say, two hundred a month. And you'd take orders from me."

Diamond laughed aloud.

Getting annoyed, Blair demanded, "What's so funny?"

"Two hundred a month? Hell, Blair, I'm no fool. If I hire my guns out it'll be for a cut of everything, just like everybody else."

"I see you're no fool. All right, you get a hundred a month and a cut from all we take out of town. The hundred is for pocket money."

"That's more like it. I'll give you an answer pretty soon."

"By the way, Diamond, remember my two boys had some good friends in this outfit. Naturally, if you're with us, we can overlook everything... but if you're not, well..."

"Is that a threat, Blair?"

"No, that's a promise. And put a handle on the Blair– Mr. Blair or Mr. Tyson."

Diamond rose from the chair slowly and looked straight into Blair's face. "I don't call no man mister unless he respects my name with mister. Remember, I might work for you, and, if I do, I'm a man and I'll remember you are too. Nobody pushes me too far and lives to tell about it."

The three men became tense as the black man spoke his peace.

"All right. Names don't matter. I'll expect an answer around the end of the month. That should give you plenty of time."

Before Diamond answered, Billy Ferrell said,

"That's plenty of time to figure things out and get a piece of that high yellow ass from Madam LaCall's maid."

Billy laughed, so did Red, but Blair reddened and snapped, "I'll see you, Diamond, on our side. Remember what you've got to lose."

"Only my life, but I've been prepared for that for a long time now."

"Look up that yellow gal and tell me about it. She looks like she has one that will sit up and bite," squealed Billy.

Diamond felt nothing behind the man's remark, knowing that when it came to women, all men wanted a woman. His last words were, "I'll be sure to see you fellows again."

When Diamond left, Billy was the first to speak. "Blair, I'm not telling you how to run things, but I think you'd better let that nigger go – or get him."

"What's the matter, Billy? Scared of a big, black nigger man?" sneered Texas Red.

"You ain't got enough sense to see that man is more dangerous than any of us; and, frankly, he gives me a funny feeling when he's around."

Texas Red continued laughing until Blair said, "The man's right, but I can use him. And, Red, in case you really don't have enough sense to know it, Diamond's more dangerous than a pit of cobras and gun powder put together."

"You fellows make me sick, scared of a nigger."

"We ain't scared, Red," yelled Billy. "That nigger don't let you know if he's mad or not. Besides, that laugh of his... he laughs at fear. He's not just a born killer like us; he's worse. He can kill you and will kill you without ever giving you any idea. He's fearless. I've seen one of his kind before. They only come in that mold once in a great while, and we've got two in town—him and Clay."

Billy shook his head in wonder and continued, "Besides," he said, "He's not sneaky like Mex or Half-Breed. He's got nerves of iron and a heart of steel. Nothing excites him. He'll kill you with his eyes. Hell, Red, didn't you see what he did last night? He's a gunman whose heart you can't take. Red, you know yourself your edge is in causing a man to doubt when you're facing him. With this bastard you never know how he's thinking."

Texas Red laughed harder than before and said, "We'll see how tough he is."

"He ain't tough, Red, that's the point. He's gentle. That's the hellfire part you…"

"Come on, let's go get something to eat," Blair cut in. He didn't want an argument between his two best men, and he sure as hell didn't want to hear Billy mention Madam LaCall's maid again.

TEN

Diamond left the town boss knowing that Clay was right and had foreseen the results of last night before he had. After he left, he knew he would never belong to Blair's outfit. But to keep them guessing for a week or so would help him and Clay fortify their positions. In any event, it bought them both a little time, at least until the end of the month.

Diamond looked up at the sun and entered, for the first time, into the Payday Casino. A quiet hush descended over the place, as if impending doom hung overhead. He ordered a drink and was served. Unnoticed by him was the look the bartender had given Kate. Her nod had said it was okay to serve him.

Kate usually, in her own way, made small talk with a new customer. She didn't with the big Negro. She had her reasons after she'd seen him last night. She'd flet the same fear that Pet had felt about Clay. And, knowing herself, she refused to give vent to any association with the man.

Clay, sitting at a table with Kate, called Diamond over. Kate scowled at Clay after he introduced Diamond saying, "Kate is the owner of this fine establishment and she serves a good brand of whiskey."

Diamond was reserved in his acknowledgement. Kate sat there, trying hard to keep her eyes from meeting the Negro's eyes. She made an excuse to leave by saying; "I'll see you men of leisure later. I've got to check on my girls, you know." After she said it, she knew it was an outward implication. She became self-conscious and felt goose pimples cover her arms.

Both Diamond and Clay stood up as she left the table and went upstairs.

"She's a nice person after you get to know her. Don't let her scare you."

"All women scare me," remarked Diamond.

Clay laughed, then anxiously inquired, "How did the meeting go with Blair?"

"Not bad, if you consider one hundred a month pocket money and a cut from the take, whatever that is."

"Oh, so they really want you, eh?"

Diamond laughed and answered, "Two ways, they tell me. I have the choice of joining or some of the friends of the dearly departed might have something in their minds like revenge. They also said I had nothing to worry about from the marshal so long as I joined up with them."

Clay became serious, letting his smile fade. "What's your answer?"

"I told them I'd think it over and let them know by the end of the month. I said I needed time." He laughed as he looked at Clay. Clay knew what his answer would be.

"Well, let's have a smoke. And, say, do you know anything about cows? I can get you a job at a dairy I'm going to invest in. It's Pet's father's place. I'm sure he'd be glad to have you."

"That's good. I'll take it."

Kate found that she couldn't stay hidden upstairs. Even the girls were saying how much of a man they believed the big black to be. Each in turn wondering who, if anyone, would get him first. "After all, money knows no color and neither does a lay," said one of the girls.

Kate was listening and trying to hide her feelings when one of the girls said, "Hell, girls, we forgot about the boss lady. Maybe he'd rather have her first. Look how pretty she is, her shape would make any man's short arm stand up fast."

The girls laughed, but to Kate it was no joke. She snapped, "LeeLee, you've known me a long time and you should know that no nigger can do anything for me. I've nothing personal against a black man, but that doesn't mean I'd let one lay me!"

"I'm sorry, Kate. I was only fooling."

Kate felt sorry for the sharpness of her words and said, "That's all right, LeeLee, maybe it would change my luck."

"Hell," said LeeLee, "that's what the black whores say when they meet a white man."

Kate chased all of them out of the room, then went to the mirror and looked at herself. She saw herself as a fine looking woman. Her black hair showed no vestige of gray; her skin was clear and smooth. She looked at her figure and smiled, knowing that it was in good shape. She was pleased with herself, thinking, "No nigger in the world would know what to do with something as nice as this." Kate added a touch of perfume to her ear and smiled. She thought, "Now, if Clay would only ask, I would." She knew this was impossible because Clay had his mind too set on Pet. She said aloud, "That sweet little bitch!"

Kate had become disgusted as her mind went from Clay to Pet to the Negro. With a resigned sigh, she returned to her bar, and she poured herself a stiff drink. She didn't return to the table where she'd left Clay and Diamond but chose, instead, to stay behind the bar. Here she could be protected from herself, at least until Clay and his black friend left.

Out at the Phillips ranch, Pet had decided to come back to town early. She wanted to do some shopping at Madam LaCall's shop and get a few things that would please Clay. Her mind had been on him all day, and she wanted more of the pleasure that she had received now that she knew what a woman was and how she felt. She had left instructions for the foreman, Pete, to see that the milk, cheese and butter were put in the springhouse for shipment into Leadville and Denver on the following morning. Usually Pet came to the ranch early and didn't leave until everything was ready for the next milking. She knew now maybe different arrangements would have to be made.

Riding towards town, the same old trail took on a new beauty. The weeds suddenly appeared as pretty wildflowers and the beaming sun gave her a tanning she could appreciate, rather than curse for its heat. She took notice of all the things around her, things that had never crossed her mind before. Birds chirping on the limbs of green trees put a song in her heart. She found the grass greener and the lofty mountains of the surrounding distance beautiful in the tranquil splendor. Her feelings about life in general changed, just as she had changed. The trees, standing tall and gently swaying with the breeze, made her think of all things great and small bowing to their maker.

"Clay, I love you for making me see the world this way," she thought.

As she rode, intently thinking of Clay, she stopped her horse to rest for a few minutes. It became apparent to her why some women rode horses so much and she smiled at the naughty idea. Calming her mind about Clay, she began to think of the things she'd buy, all of them pretty.

The ride didn't take long. She put her horse away and headed for Madam LaCall's shop. The Madam helped her select some French undergarments, a couple of feminine blouses, two nighties of sheer material and three riding shirts, one red, one yellow and one light blue.

She admired herself in the mirror. She noticed the difference of how her long golden hair, along with the new things, made her a beautiful picture of a happy woman. She'd even worn a pair of undergarments, something she hardly ever did. Pleased with her looks, she rubbed her hips admiringly and went to find Clay.

Kate was standing behind the bar having just said goodbye to Clay and Diamond. They had missed seeing Pet by only a few seconds. Kate froze when Pet walked in.

"Gee, your baby looks good, Kate," called the girl LeeLee.

Kate felt a shudder go through her body. Without saying a word, she moved upstairs with Pet close behind her. When they were in Kate's room, Pet felt a coolness from her and, feeling ill, asked, "What's wrong, Kate?"

"Nothing. Why?"

"At least you could tell me how good I look, after the hell you gave me about clothes before."

"I'm sorry, Pet. I'm not myself today."

Kate knew she was being cold to Pet. Pet, with her carefree self, removed her boots as she often did. Kate didn't stop her. Pet pranced in front of the mirror, giving Kate a full show of her inviting hips.

"Well, how do you like it? Do you see a change in me?"

Kate looked at her closely for the first time. "I'd say your eyes are sparkling for some reason, and there's a little sadness to your face."

"Then congratulate me. I got it," laughed Pet.

"Got what?" Kate asked puzzled.

The young girl became coy and shy.

"Oh," gasped Kate, "you mean Clay got you."

"That he did, Kate, and it was beautiful – a beautiful thing. I ended up like a stuck pig."

Kate laughed at her awkwardness in telling things so frankly, yet she felt relieved at Pet's welfare. "Well, now you're a woman."

"Sure I am. I know now what a woman's for. And, Kate, I'm so happy."

Pet put her arm around Kate's waist. Kate anxiously, knowing Pet would not leave anything out, said, "Tell me about it."

Pet told her everything.

Kate gasped, "Pet, you aren't supposed to tell that part; it's too personal."

Pet looked up at her with an innocent gaze. "I don't know why I can't tell you, Kate. After all, you loved me enough to do it, so I loved him enough."

Kate understood, but wondered about herself. She explained, "Pet, baby, there are other things I meant to tell you. Now, since you're not a virgin anymore but a full woman, I'll tell you. Always take care of the lower part of your body. You'll never know when he'll want it so always keep it fresh. Wash your face a couple of times a day, but wash that," she said as she pointed, "much more often. That's the secret of a woman's charm."

Kate was feeling partly herself now, but not for long. The two women discussed what had happened to Clay the night before. Pet revealed to Kate that Diamond had stayed in the hotel, and then she remarked, "He sure is a cool one, that Diamond."

"Yeah, he is. I wonder just how cool he is," spoke Kate.

"Well, I really should be going, Kate. I just came down to..."

Kate noticed the long pause and asked, "To what?"

"To... oh, never mind. You don't want..."

"Want what, Pet?"

"I thought you didn't want to do that again?"

"Pet, baby, I do!" said Kate, "But it's not right. And you shouldn't want me now that you've got Clay."

"Maybe not, but I remember what you told me, that a piece of tail is like a hog's nose.

No matter how much you use it, you can't wear it out, and there's always enough left to satisfy anybody who wants some."

"You remember too damned much. And why do you still want me, Pet? The only reason I did it the first time was because, as hot as you were, with a little smooth talk Blair or any one of that bunch could have had you."

"Thanks, Kate, maybe you're right. The way I felt, if you hadn't have done what you did; I'd have done it with anyone. And the reason I want it again is because I like it and I like you. I've got to try and keep you and Clay happy, at least until you find a man you want."

"Well, you needn't be so blunt. Anyway, I think I've found my man, but it's just my luck the bastard is black!"

Pet screamed with amazement, "You mean that ni..."

"Yeah, I mean that nigger!"

"Well, in that case, I won't be coming around so often."

"I didn't say that, you did. But put yourself at ease, I won't be carrying on with Diamond because that black son of a bitch doesn't even know I'm alive."

Pet laughed. This made Kate a little angry and she snapped, "It's not a damned bit funny."

"I know. That's why I'm laughing," said Pet, removing her blouse .

Kate came to her as before. This time Pet stood in the middle of the floor as Kate undressed her. Kate gazed with renewed admiration at the young girl's nude, almost boyish body. Pet felt Kate and she quivered. Pet went over to the bed as Kate undressed, revealing her nude body to Pet for the first time. Pet was astonished and exclaimed, "God, you're as beautiful as I am."

Kate lay beside her and put her arms around her neck. Kate kissed her body as before.

Kate finished her work with a hurting pleasure that made her sink in a jerking motion from the torment taking place within her. "You made me do it again."

Kate's words went unheard, for Pet had fainted. Cold water returned her to consciousness. She immediately put her arms around Kate and kissed her.

"That's the last time ever, understand Pet?"

Pet said, "Okay, this is the last time."

ELEVEN

Diamond and Clay separated. Diamond went to the bank and the general store while Clay took the opposite direction. He passed Madam LaCall's shop and noticed that the Negro maid was watching him. A smile followed.

Down the street Clay saw the people he was looking for, Blair Tyson, Texas Red Morgan and Hank. All three were going into the jail. A sardonic smile crossed Clay's face. He looked up at the flat-roofed buildings as he passed and crossed the street to the jail. The men and Blair were in the midst of a small sort of discussion when suddenly the door of the jail flew open with a bang. Standing there, the men saw Clay for the first time as a U.S. Marshal. Their quick eyes swept over him from head to foot, seeing all, especially the tied-down authority. They were a paired group. Clay quickly counted seven rough-looking men in need of a shave and a bath. Clay had seen them all before, but his presence here now was official business. Blair, seated on a chair with his feet on the desk, showed no surprise at the lawman. Neither did any of the others.

Clay's voice thundered with a keen sharpness, "I'm

glad I found all of you together. It saves me the trouble of telling you each separately what I have to say."

"What's on your mind, Marshal? Say it and get. We've got things to talk about," remarked Blair.

Clay had sized up the gang and didn't take his eyes off of them as he moved inside the door.

"Hell, damned if it ain't true; he's the law," said Texas Red.

"Yeah," said Mex, making an ugly snarl. "You should've shot him when you first started, Red."

"Sure would have saved a hell of a lot of trouble," said one of the others.

"Well, he looks all right after his little bloomer party," said Billy. They all roared with laughter.

Clay took out his cigarettes and lit one.

"Hey, let us try one of those ready-rolled, Marshal. After all, we ain't got no hard feelings against you," Hank said.

Clay tossed the pack on the desk and watched them take one and light up. Only Blair refused, saying, "I believe the Marshal is a right smart lawman. Being he's just one man, I feel he's learned his lesson about meddling into things that don't concern him." He looked at Clay questionably.

Billy Ferrell then spoke. "He knows we were only teasing him the other night, but now, since he's a U.S. Marshal... Hey, Breed, what ever happened to that last lawman we had?"

"Somebody found him cut to pieces like a butchered steer. I thought you knew that, Billy," answered Breed.

Those remarks were meant, as Clay knew, to intimidate him and to see if he could be bought. Or maybe they were just plain warnings. However they were meant, Clay's face remained stern as he listened. He shifted his weight and said, "All right, you've had your fun and your say. Now, listen to me. By noon tomorrow I want this jail cleaned out or else I'll burn anything I find here. Now, as for your little party the other night, I've decided there will be another one; only this time I'm giving it. I saved the pink bloomers and I'm serving you each a piece of them right down your lousy throats, starting with you Blair."

No one spoke and Clay continued, "As of Monday, the first of the week, there will be no more guns worn in a saloon."

"What the hell is this?" cried Texas Red.

"You heard me. There will be checkpoints in each saloon. Leave them there. Otherwise, it's thirty days in jail or a fifty dollar fine."

"I give my guns to nobody," argued Texas Red.

"Then I'll take them," answered Clay. "That's just what I want you to do, resist so I can kill you. I've got a personal reason for killing you, Red. Any way you look at it, your time is running out."

The men looked at Texas Red to see what he would do.

Blair raised his hand. "That's not so bad, Marshal. I'm glad to see you on the job, but keep your nose out of our affairs."

"And just what are your affairs?"

"Practically everything in town, so you have a very narrow road to travel. Don't slip."

Clay's eyes burned into Blair's. "I've had my say, now get out of here and carry all your gear with you. You're on state and county property."

"All right, boys, get your things. But about that property business, you'll see whose property it is," remarked Blair.

Clay knew that Blair had made a reference to the land grant but said nothing. The rest of the men grumbled as they went past him, carrying objects and extra guns, saddles and bridles. Billy Ferrell was the last to leave. He was carrying a heavy rifle. Clay looked at the gun and moved in front of Billy saying, "Let's see that rifle," catching the man by surprise. Clay took the rifle and saw it was a .44-.70.

Outside, the rest of the gang had stopped, all looking back towards Clay and Billy. Clay carefully examined the heavy rifle and saw that it was loaded. He held the gun and fired it into the corner of the room, then removed the spent shell. He looked at the firing pin mark on the shell and withdrew from his pocket the same kind of shell. Examining the evidence, Clay found what he had already suspected to be true: the off center dent in the primer was the same.

"You're under arrest, Billy."

"What the hell for?"

"For killing Phillips' bull."

"The damned fool!" Clay heard Texas Red say.

Blair stopped in the door. "What are you keeping Billy for? I'm his lawyer."

"I don't give a damn who you are. I caught him with the rifle that killed Phillips' bull so I'm locking up my first customer."

Blair said nothing, only looked daggers at Billy.

Clay took Billy's guns and moved him into a dirty cell, slammed the door and locked it with the rusty key that was sticking out of the lock.

"What are you gonna do?" asked Blair.

"Nothing until Phillips comes back to town. I'll ask him what he wants. No doubt Billy will have to pay for the bull."

"You know you have to prove a case against him."

"I've proven it."

"Not to satisfy me, you haven't," answered Blair.

"The hell with you. I'm interested in satisfying Mr. Phillips, so no smart lawyer tricks until he pays."

Blair stormed from the room feeling defeated and knowing Clay had a cold case against Billy and couldn't be buffaloed. He huddled with the others as Clay stood in the door and looked on, paying no attention to Billy who was shouting, "Get me the hell out of here, Blair."

It was a busy day for Clay. He spent the rest of the day visiting shops and telling folks of the changes he'd made. From Mr. Graystone Clay had found a man to act as a swamper for the jail and run errands for ten dollars a month. Everyone knew the man as "Old John". He seemed to know what was required of him. Clay also visited the two saloons and told them about the new town ordinance to check all guns at the door. The owners were more than pleased and happy to comply. Mr. Graystone had informed him that the decent people were behind him and that an election was coming up for a mayor and a town judge.

During his travels, Clay hadn't seen Diamond. A few people had inquired about the Negro most favorably, which indicated a passive kind of acceptance.

Clay had a glimpse of Pet, he thought, but couldn't be sure. Pet had seen him from a store window and her heart had done turnovers.

The biggest thing on Clay's mind now was disposing of the Billy Ferrell affair. Because there was no courthouse or schoolhouse, he'd asked Kate if he could hold a hearing of sorts there when Phillips returned. She'd agreed. Then Clay had asked Old John to tell as many men as he could to be present Monday for the hearing at the Payday where the makeshift court would be held. He also told folks to pass the word along, and they did, knowing that they now had a leader who would bring order to the chaotic town of Pueblo.

It had been a few days since Clay had sent his wire to his uncle Mart in Austin, and as of yet, no answer had returned. Just to be sure, Clay checked with the telegraph operator.

It was just past 4 pm. Clay hung around the small station waiting until the 4:20 train came in. He saw Madam LaCall's maid come into the station. He noticed how high she carried herself and how her coarse black hair glistened in the sunlight. He thought about Diamond, saying to himself, "Diamond could sure play hell with that. Or maybe he already has."

He spoke to the maid and she returned his greeting. A conversation was started by him asking, "You ain't taking a trip are you, Emma?"

Her voice was soft and seductive. "Yes, Marshal, I'm going to Denver for the Madam."

"Well, don't be gone too long, the town will miss you."

"Only a few days and I'll return," she smiled.

"By the way, there's a friend of mine in town who'd like to meet you I think."

"Meet me? Now who could that be?" she said.

"You'll see him around, no doubt."

She knew who he was talking about, but her mind

was in an utterly different direction that afternoon. "Oh, well, when I see him what is it he'll want?"

Clay blushed and said, "He'll have to tell you that for himself." Clay could have said more but the train, with its steaming boiler, came to a squealing halt, throwing cinders all over people. A few people got off; but none Clay knew.

Emma got on the train saying, "Come see me at the shop, Marshal. It just might brighten your future days."

The remark was pointed and Clay answered, "I just might do that, Emma," and thought to himself, "A whole damn town full of skins, a single man's paradise."

The train pulled out, making even more noise than when it had stopped. Clay found that he had no package or wire, then walked back across town to his office in the jail. He'd been in his office only a little while, just long enough to see that Billy was still secure in his cell sleeping, when Pet filled the doorway. His face showed he was pleased. She threw herself in his arms, and felt him in her own way.

"Hi, Marshal."

"Hi," is all Clay could manage to say, holding her and feeling the rapture from her touch.

She stood back to look down at the rising results and said, "I always want to see and know that you want me."

He looked at her red blouse, taking in the full shape of her body in the outfit and was filled with pleasure.

TWELVE

The job of Marshal had no regular hours. It was a twenty-four hour job, the days always beginning early and ending late. With his first full day, things had gone well for Clay. He looked at his watch and felt the need for food. He wondered where Diamond had been all day as he wandered over to the hotel to eat. The day, drawing to a close, still had a brightness. It would be at least three hours before dark would settle over the town. Clay had waited until Old John had returned to inform him that he would be at the hotel until later if anything came up. After Clay left, the old man locked the door and settled in the old rocking chair, which was a pretty good place for napping.

Clay had dinner with Pet. She served him, beaming as she sat across from him. People in the dining room managed to keep their heads before them until Diamond made his appearance. Clay never moved but watched the others in the room as Pet called out for Diamond to come over the table and join them. Pet never thought what results might follow her actions. She didn't seem to care what others thought.

Clay asked, "Where have you been hiding all day?"

Diamond revealed he'd been on the river fishing and had spent the day camping out. Clay made no issue of the respite but, in turn, told Diamond about the jail meeting and what he'd told Blair and Texas Red.

During the conversation Pet told Diamond he could have the dairy job. When Diamond said he'd seen the ranch, Pet laughed. "Scouting already?"

Diamond showed his teeth.

Clay told them both the big news about the new gun law starting Monday.

Diamond said, "I'll be working at the dairy."

Clay had to laugh at the sly way Diamond evaded his order. Pet told Diamond that her father would be back tomorrow night and that he could move out to the ranch on Sunday, "Unless, she said like a pixie, "you intend on seeing Madam LaCall's maid."

Clay could see Diamond's face and said, "She went to Denver, I saw her when she was leaving this afternoon. Anyway, I'm sure Diamond can find something else to do."

Diamond had refused food but took a cigarette from Clay and with a yawn said, "Think I'll mosey down to the Payday and then turn in early."

Clay could tell the man was in need of something to occupy his mind. He said, "I'll see you down there for a few hands of poker."

"Just give me your money now," said Diamond, smiling subtly.

"Hell, you ain't that good," declared Clay, finishing his meal.

Clay kissed Pet before leaving and she whispered, "Hurry back. This is the last night before Dad comes home and I'm dying for some more."

She thought she was whispering, but Diamond had heard her. She caught his eye and blushed. She said, "Well, what the hell are you grinning about? I'll bet you've found a hole to play in, or you're thinking about one anyhow."

Diamond laughed. So did Clay. But Clay blushed and shook Pet saying, "I'm going to wash your mouth out with soap. I'll see you later."

Catching up to Diamond, he said, "She's a good woman, but she's a mess."

"She's a wonderful girl, Clay, and I hanker to say you're a good man. Keep her satisfied with what she wants and you'll always have her."

"Yeah, if I don't break my back first."

"Hey, Marshal, I'd like to see you for a few minutes," someone called.

Clay crossed over to talk to the man while Diamond continued on to the Payday Casino alone.

Kate, sitting at her regular table, moved behind the bar when she saw the Negro coming in. He ordered a drink, quickly downed it and waited for the bartender to return his change from the twenty dollar gold piece. The place was crowded as usual, but the rough-looking men took no particular interest in him.

Along the back wall near the gambling tables, stood Blair, Texas Red and Hank, while two others whom Blair used sat at a table talking to the girls. Kate's eyes moved from Diamond to Blair and on to Texas Red, not that she sensed trouble but because she felt hatred for the black man who now stood watching the poker game.

One of the girls whispered something to her working friend and both girls began watching Kate. Her eyes were wide in a sort of stare, almost dreamy. Her body was taut.

"I'm going to put that nigger through the races tonight. All of the boys are here, just in case," Hank told Blair.

Blair gave the okay. He wanted to get even with Clay for arresting Billy and for putting the new gun law into play.

Blair said, "Buy him in a card game, and if you have to shoot, kill the black bastard. I think Billy was right, that nigger is too dangerous."

Hank only nodded.

This order was given because Blair had thought about the remark Billy made about Madam LaCall's yellow maid and he figured from that alone he would have trouble out of Diamond. His biggest gripe was that in their talk that morning the black had actually laughed at him. He had brooded over this all day, knowing that if the man had any intention of working for him, he'd have said so then. Blair moved over to Texas Red and told him to squeeze Diamond if trouble started and to back Hank's play.

All the while the men shifted and talked while Diamond watched from the corner of his eyes, half shielded by the wide brim of his hat. The big brown Negro made up his mind right then that he was to be the target of a cold setup. He also figured he might as well tell Blair tonight that he wasn't going to be working for him. He laughed to himself, "Guess he already knows that."

Texas Red moved to the table directly in front of the table where the girls sat, where he'd have room to move, just in case. There was a small game going on.

Hank took a seat and called out, "Diamond, come

on over here, you bastard. I want to take your money
from you."

The Negro, moving slowly, approached the table,
getting a good layout of where the others were. Naturally, Blair pulled up a chair.

"Sit down. Ain't nobody gonna bite you," said Hank.

"Hank, you haven't got enough of me yet? And what
are you doing, Blair, seeing if I can handle my money?"
Diamond asked.

"That's right. We don't want any of the boys being
to careless with money, especially big money like you'll
be handling."

Diamond knew he had thrown them off the track,
and he had to keep them that way until they made their
play.

When Cliff Diamond sat down, no one noticed that
he had loosened his guns so that the least rocking
motion he made would cause them to tumble out. Nobody, that is, but Kate. She saw his every move. She
felt that sickening feeling again, remembering what she
had conveyed to Pet about the black man. She knew
why she hated him, and felt the sooner they killed him,
or he moved out of town, the better off she'd be.

Clay entered the saloon, nodded to Kate and, seeing that Diamond was busy, took a position leaning
against the bar to watch the game. He also saw the others stacked in position and felt a fearfulness for Diamond. But something told him the Negro knew. Diamond looked up from the table and Clay caught the
message in his eyes and returned a knowing grin to
show he understood.

At the table sat Hank, a miner, a drummer, Blair
and Diamond.

Hank said, "Open game, dealer's choice, no holds barred and the sky's the limit. Can't play; give your seat to someone who can. Agreed, men?"

Although he was at the table, Blair was not in the game. He sat slightly behind Hank with the miner on his right.

Hank shuffled the pasteboards after all had agreed to the rules. He dealt five-card stud, two dollars in the pot. All stayed for the ante. He passed the cards around, the first one face down. Diamond looked at his hole card, a king of hearts.

The second came face up; it was a queen. He bet. Diamond then caught a ten spot and folded. Hank laughed, and, after the hand, he drew in the pot. On the next deal Diamond stayed, playing a pair of tens. On the last card he was called and raised; he called. The miner tried a bluff. Diamond dealt the third game and folded after the second card. The drummer gave up his seat, saying it was getting too rough for him. The deal went around until it got to Hank again. He winked, coughed and said, "Diamond, near catch consumption in here."

"That and TB, too," echoed Diamond, laughing at his own joke. He still kept them from knowing that he knew it was a setup.

Hank shuffled and started to deal.

"Set them down, Hank, I want to cut."

A hard look crossed Hank's face.

Now, from where Clay stood he saw the swift stack Hank had made; so did Diamond. But when Diamond cut, he also carried an inner stack to the deck. Hank dealt, each man staying until the last card was dealt.

Diamond looked at the table.

Hank said, "Possible straight bets."

That was the miner, he bet; and Diamond only called with his ten, jack, queen and king of hearts showing. Hank had what he had stacked. A straight flush in sequence: six, seven, eight and nine with his ten in the hole. Hank called and raised fifty dollars. The miner folded and removed himself, leaving only Diamond and Hank. Diamond called and raised three hundred, throwing a stack of gold pieces into the pot.

Hank looked at him. "You can't bluff me, boy. I'll even call." He then counted out three hundred dollars and pushed it forward, making the pot over seven hundred dollars.

"Hell, Hank, I thought you had nerve. Why don't you raise?"

"I do raise, a hundred dollars more," snarled Hank.

Diamond knew he had riled him and knew he was flustered. Counting out five twenty dollar gold pieces he said, "I'll just call you, Hank.

Hank turned over his hole card showing the straight flush.

Diamond laughed. "Brother, you ain't got enough," he said as he turned over his hole card, an ace of hearts.

Hank looked at the Negro and declared, "I never did trust a black nigger anyhow."

"Me either," replied Diamond. "Any time a white man – trash like you – tries to run a cold deck on me, I go right behind him, you polecat of a cheat."

The room was quiet. Hank wanted to draw, knowing he had help, but Diamond's words stung him. "You stupid, white bastard, can't you see Blair wants to get you killed?" But I'm not going to satisfy him by killing you – not now, anyway. But draw and I'll cut you down like a dog. And you, Red, don't take another step unless you're ready to go to hell fast," said Diamond, having total command of the situation. He knew Clay had his back covered from the two men at the table behind him.

Then Diamond spoke sternly, "Blair, understand this: I wouldn't work for you if you were paying a million. I may be black, but I'm not a crook, nor do I gather with a pack. But you and your wolves have got your cap set to get me. Well, go ahead, draw. And wake up in hell." Then he added, "And you, Texas Red, you son of a bitch, I want you to draw. I don't care what a man calls me to my face, but I hate a bastard like you who degrades a man behind his back. I'm warning every one of you – and the law is here to hear this – cross my path once more and I'll kill the bunch of you. I'm not looking for trouble, but I won't run from it either."

There wasn't a sound. Kate's heart was in her mouth. Hank didn't know what to do. He just said, "All right, nigger, you called it this time but the next time we meet somebody's going to hell."

Blair saw his whole gang up against it and told Hank to cool down. But he couldn't stand the Negro insulting him. He walked to the door, turned and flashed. Diamond fired two well-placed shots, one in each shoulder, causing Hank to wheel around from the impact of the bullets and curse, "You black son of a bitch, I'll kill you for breaking my arms."

Diamond looked at him calmly and said, "That's why I busted them, so, if you've got any brains, you'll remember never to pack guns again, especially against me."

The remainder of Blair's gang filed out, keeping

their eyes focused on Diamond and carrying their fallen comrade with them.

Clay had no need to touch his guns. Diamond walked over to the drummer and said, "Here's your money back. That was a rigged game." He also returned the miner's money.

Clay waited until he ordered a drink then said, "You had me scared there for a second. I thought you were going to kill him."

"I should have. But I'll let you do that. He hates your guts about as much as mine."

When his drink was finished, Diamond said, "Had you not been here to see what happened, I would have had to kill him."

"I saw what he did. But how did you stop him?"

"That's a long story, Clay. After I saw him pull his bug, I just upped him."

"You know quite a bit for a man just looking for someone."

"Clay, I'll tell you something. When you are in my position, you get to know a little bit about a lot of things and know them damn well enough to come out on top."

"I guess you're right, Cliff. But how in the hell can you keep them all off you now?"

Diamond reflected a second and said, "Let's worry about that when the time comes, Marshal."

THIRTEEN

Diamond left the Payday without telling Clay where he was going. He wanted to be alone to think out a few things. He walked down to the river and dug out a fishing pole he'd hidden in the thickets from his previous fishing trip.

With his line out, he sat on the riverbank thinking of everything that had taken place since he'd first ridden into Pueblo and rescued Clay from the bloomer bash that Blair's men had been giving him. Diamond's thoughts ended with the poker game that Blair had set him up for.

Suddenly he reached out and grabbed his pole, jerking it from the water. After taking off the two-pound catfish, he had just recast his line into the moonlit water when his keen ears picked up the sound of a breaking twig nearby.

He quietly laid down the pole and stood tense, listening and waiting. His dry hands hovered near the cherry butts of his guns, ready to spring into action spitting out instant death in any direction.

Again the sound came, this time from the right side. With the speed of a striking rattler, he spun, guns leaping into the palms of his waiting hands. He peered into the darkness from where the sound had come. A shadowy form stepped out from behind a tree into the moonlight. Diamond showed surprise and relief as he recognized one of the girls that worked at the Payday.

He holstered his guns saying angrily, "What the hell are you doing here, girl? Don't you realize I might have killed you sneaking up on me like that?"

"I didn't mean to alarm you. I just wanted to talk to you."

"Talk? What do you want to talk to me about?"

Walking slowly up to him, with her eyes taking in everything they saw in this man, she replied, "Oh, I don't know. I watched you back in the Payday and when you left I followed you here."

"Why?"

"I thought you might be lonesome."

She was standing right next to him now, and Diamond noticed the loveliness of the girl before him. Her high breasts jutted out in twin peaks from underneath her blouse, and her slender hips had the inviting curves that promised better things upon inspection.

She put her arms around him and pressed her body tightly against him. Her hand traveled down his belt and felt tighter against Diamond as she whispered,

"Come on, Diamond, let's hurry. I don't want Kate to miss me."

Again she reached down and pulled him. Diamond took her by the hand and led her towards the darkness of the trees.

Later, when Diamond had gone to bed, Clay was restless in his room, thinking of how much trouble was headed his way and knowing that Hank wouldn't be satisfied until he either killed Diamond or vice-versa. Yet Clay figured he had the best solution. He'd keep Diamond out at the dairy ranch, or try to force him to leave town for his own good. He realized the latter wouldn't work, but determined to give it a try.

A soft rap on Clay's door broke his chain of thought. He asked, "Who's there?"

"Open the door," a soft voice whispered.

Clay opened the door and Pet slipped in wearing a flimsy white night gown. Clay wasn't too surprised, but a little leery.

"Well, don't you want me?" she asked pouting.

He answered by putting his arms around her and nuzzling her breasts.

Feeling his naked body and his panting she said, "Umm, that feels good, Clay. Rip this damn gown off me!"

He looked at her.

"Go ahead, rip it off. I want you to."

He grabbed the front of the delicate fabric and, with strength in his fingers, tore the gown into pieces from her body. The sound of the rending material caused her to panic with delight. The effect gave him an added zest to have her. He looked at whiteness, standing with the torn gown at her feet. She came to him in a submissive manner. He carried her to the bed where he showered her with kisses.

Pet whispered, "We'll have to make this last. Dad will be back tomorrow."

He didn't answer until he felt her go limp under him. Then he said, "I could eat you up."

Through her frantic breathing she replied, "I wish you would. God, I do!"

From the contracting twists of her body being torn into by the force of his lips upon her, her pleas to him had been answered. Together, the rest of the night was a quietness of peace in each other's arms.

***

Blair Tyson had his men with him in his office. They had doctored Hank the best they could; both arms were busted. That would make him more uncomfortable than anything else. They had found and removed the ugly slugs and wrapped him in a swath of bandages. Blair decided one of his men could help take care of Hank until he could get around. He detailed the job to Stoker, one of his stooge gunmen. The men were in a nasty mood, especially Texas Red who wanted to just hunt Diamond down and kill him.

Blair managed to calm him down. "We'll all take a hand in that after we pull this train job. That's the important thing now."

"Hell, if Diamond and that nigger loving marshal keep going, there won't be nobody left to do the job," blurted Red.

Blair cast him a dirty look. "We'll have Billy back Monday. That will help."

"How do you know for sure?" asked the Mex.

"He'll probably just be fined for the price of the bull, that's all. It's no hell of a big case. Then we sit tight until after the first." He rubbed his chin and continued, "After that, you can blow the hell out of this town, and anybody else with it, for all I care."

"I'll go along with that. But does that thousand dollars still go if that black son of a bitch gets killed?"

"Listen, Breed, that marshal ain't no fool. And he's pure hell himself. He'll back the law against his own mother. If anything happens to that nigger bastard before Hank gets well, everything points to us. Look around. Can't you see the town is siding with the marshal?"

Blair made his point effectively. The men grumbled, but it was the prospect of the big haul keeping their guns off the marshal and Cliff Diamond, at least for now.

***

After the thunder of Diamond's guns had died down, Kate found herself a bundle of nerves. She went to her room, telling LeeLee to look after things. She undressed and splashed cold water over herself, feeling refreshed. She dried off and sat at the mirror, letting her hair down. The long black tresses flowed to her shoulders. She combed her hair and reset it atop her head. Her thoughts were all mixed up. She blew out the lamp and lay naked across the bed. The light of the moon threw a hazy shadow across the room. In her thinking, she dozed off to sleep. A rap at the door awakened her.

"Who is it?" she asked.

"LeeLee," a voice said.

"Come on in, it isn't locked."

LeeLee entered and, seeing her boss naked on the bed asked, "Are you that tired, Kate?"

"Yeah. I got here and couldn't go any further."

"Well, everything is put away. Caroline is out some place, but the joint is closed. It's been a really busy day. Is there anything I can do for you before I go to bed?"

"Yes. Sit down for a minute. I want to ask you something."

LeeLee sat down and crossed her legs, hiking her short dress over her knees. She looked at Kate, wondering what she wanted.

Kate looked at her, smiled and spoke, "I ain't got the strength to cover myself."

"That's all right with me. You've got the kind of body that makes the little man in the boat sweat. Besides, we women are a common lot anyway."

Kate moved her head, and through the dimness saw LeeLee's crossed legs. "Damn, LeeLee, don't tell me you're that way."

"Uh-huh. A man ain't nothing but a man, but a woman ain't nothing but a bitch without one, and Kate, I ain't got one."

"LeeLee, what I wanted to ask you is, how long have you been in this business?"

"Ever since my mother told me not to give it away."

"And have you ever given any away since?" Kate laughed.

"A few times when the man was real good," sighed LeeLee dreamingly.

Kate turned over on her side facing the girl. "Any niggers in the bunch?"

"A few now and then. Why?"

"Nothing. I'm just curious."

"You really want to know how they act? I'll tell you, Kate," the girl said rubbing her hips. "Once you've had one, you'll never forget it. God, Kate, they're like sugar in a way; hard but fine. Once you get a bit of it, too much will kill you. The craving is always there. Believe me, Kate, they're real nice."

"Hell, they can't be nice," scorned Kate.

"That's what you think! A black man needs a white

woman and a white man needs a black bitch. Why, I don't know, but I know a nigger whore who went crazy over a white man. I had the same guy and so did the other girls, and we all agreed he wasn't worth a snake's ass."

"Why, LeeLee?"

"Well, for one reason, a white man's nature is quick, so is a Negro woman's. And a white woman's is longer, so is the black man's. And you can bet some white women get plenty, one way or the other, so does a white man; but, because of this black and white rule, both races suffer."

"Jesus, LeeLee, I'm older than you, but you know more than I do."

LeeLee shrugged her shoulders. "Kate, in this business I've had women and men of both races, with all kinds of wants. I should know something."

"Tell me, LeeLee, would you choose a white man over a nigger?"

"Frankly, Kate, I'll have one and sneak around to get some of the other. The difference is what a woman wants!"

"LeeLee, you gave me reasons for hating this Diamond. I know now he'll never get none of this."

"Wanna bet, Kate? You fool the other whores, but you don't fool me. I hated one, too, because he didn't pay me no mind. Then, when I did get him, the bastard nearly screwed me out of my mind."

"Are you serious?"

"Hell, yes. And let me give you some advice, Kate. You keep right on hating that curly headed black bastard because if he ever gets them pretty thighs of yours, you're cooked. And I mean that."

"Don't be a fool, LeeLee. I couldn't stand a black man on top of me."

"That's what all of us white women and whores say, at the same time wanting desperately to crawl beneath one."

Kate jumped from her bed in a tempest, with her breasts bouncing in the moonlight causing LeeLee to breathe heavily.

"Kate, between you and me, you'll be all right when you can run your white fingers through that wavy black hair of Diamond's and feel that steel spring of his growing."

"Hell, I'd rather have a woman!" she replied angrily.

LeeLee stood up, went over to Kate and stood beside her. Kate turned around, seeing the girl's boldness. She lifted LeeLee's dress above her waist, knowing the dress was all she had on.

"I know how you feel, Kate. We women are bitches when we can't have what we want, but we can always have each other, beauty and all, can't we?"

"Sure, angel, sure," answered Kate.

***

The next day, when the 11:45 arrived from Denver, Mr. Phillips proudly stepped from the high coach steps. He checked with the agent of the station for mail.

"Nothing for you, Martin, but here's a wire for Marshal Clinton."

"Marshal! What Marshal?"

Mr. Phillips was agitated by the slowness with which the agent spoke. The agent in return was surprised that Mr. Phillips didn't know.

"He stays at your hotel, the fellow with the fancy

yellow vest."

Phillips was relieved to know Clay was out in the open now.

"Oh, you mean Clay."

"Yep, that's the one."

Mr. Phillips took the wire from the agent, glanced at it and put it in his coat pocket, brushing dirt from his soiled, rumpled suit. He was about to say something when he noticed the agent looking at him queerly.

"What's wrong, Ben?" he asked.

"T'ain't none of my business, but since you've been gone I think you got a new roomer at your place."

"What's so strange about that? That's what a hotel is for."

"Yep, I know, but I didn't know you put up with niggers though."

With glowing indignation, Mr. Phillips demanded, "What are you talking about?"

"I kinda figured you didn't know since this fella came after you left. And, to boot, he's raising all kinda hell; killed two of Blair's men already and shot another just last night over at the Payday."

The news jolted the hotel owner, but he had no love for Blair or his men.

"Seems to me the town should be thankful. And about a colored man living at my place of business, he evidently has his reasons for being there."

The agent took the verbal slap in the face with a pointing of his finger at Martin Phillips. "All right, that's your place, but good white folks don't have to eat and stay there with a nigger."

Mr. Phillips stormed from the station in a rage.

The day was bright and clear, with a feel of rain in

the air. Mr. Phillips mopped his brow and neck as he walked across town to see what was going on at his hotel. He tried to make sense out of what the agent had told him. He also knew that Clay was around, so he had no real cause to worry.

The people he passed in the street spoke in a cool manner and cast sly glances at him. Some even turned around to look at him after passing. The town looked the same to him, but the quiet stillness could be meant to serve as a warning; the calm before the storm. He was hailed by Mr. Graystone who was on his way to his store.

"Glad to see you back, Martin. Maybe now we can get things done."

Mr. Graystone repeated the same information the station agent had relayed. Graystone made him feel somewhat better by saying, "We are in business, Martin, and some folks just don't understand. That black fellow came into my store and bought some things. Frankly, he was easier to wait on than some whites. Anyway, the marshal is really getting things done."

"Good, glad to hear it. We can be proud of that young man."

"I understand he's got the fellow who shot your bull."

"Yeah? Who was it?"

"Billy Ferrell. You go on home and the marshal will tell you everything. And you tell the marshal we're all behind him. And, oh yeah, I almost forgot... you might be getting an addition to the family soon, too."

"How's that?"

"Pet's dressing pretty fancy, which tells me there's a special man who's caught her eye."

Mr. Phillips laughed and said to himself, "Clay, boy, you not only took over the town, but Pet, too."

Mr. Phillips again headed for his hotel, thinking now about Pet. He was remembering what it was like when he was a young man around a pretty young lady and he was trying to brush that thought from his mind. He was proud of Clay and, if what he had thought was true, he would be more than pleased to have him for a son-in-law.

He bounced up the hotel steps and the clerk behind the desk began to explain about the Negro in room 10.

"That's all right. Don't worry about it," he said.

The clerk kept explaining that it was Miss Pet's doing.

Mr. Phillips nodded his head. He saw the waitress looking at him and asked, "Well, what's on your mind, Mary?"

"Nothing. Just thought you might want something to eat."

He called out to Pet and Clay, but no one answered. Then he realized Pet was probably out at the ranch and Clay was probably out working the town.

After he'd washed up and changed his clothes, he came down the stairs and confronted a few other men who voiced their opinions concerning the town marshal and the Negro. After listening to the mild raving for the third time that day, he ended the conversation with an abrupt, "I don't care if he is black, from what I hear we should all be grateful to the man."

He walked from the room, leaving the men with red faces and their citizenship jolted. Walking down the plank sidewalk, Mr. Phillips noticed that in all the talk he'd heard so far, no one had said why the Negro had raised hell and killed two men. He was curious about this but figured if anybody knew, Clay would. But if Clay knew about the killings, why wasn't the Negro in jail?

He didn't have long to wait to receive his answer, for he saw Clay coming from the Payday Casino on his way back to his office at the jail.

Clay saw Mr. Phillips hurrying over to him and slowed his pace as the man came along side him and asked, "How are you, Clay? How are things going?"

"A little rugged. How was your trip?"

"Real fine. I got a damned good buy on an Angus. Not too young, but real serviceable."

"Good," said Clay. "Come on over to the jail, I want to talk to you."

"Here, the agent gave me this," he said, handing Clay the wire.

"Oh, yeah, thanks. I've been waiting for this."

"Clay, what's been going on around here? Everybody's talking."

"I'll tell you over at the jail."

Walking with Clay, Mr. Phillips looked him over good and close, and he liked what he saw; the full regalia of a U.S. Marshal, which, in a manly way, added stature and a reserved dignity to Clay. He matched strides with him, nodding to people and proud to be associated with him. Aside from this, he had the hopes that Clay would be the man for his daughter.

FOURTEEN

This was the first time in over two or three years, in fact it had been five years that Mr. Phillips had been inside the jail. He looked around the office while Clay read the letter from his uncle, which read:

Mr. Clay Clinton
C/O Phillips Hotel
Pueblo, Colorado
Dear Nephew,
Am forwarding clothes and cigarettes. Hope every-thing fits. Have checked land grants in the state of Colorado. There were three such grants. Am waiting reply from Washington to verify this officer's check. Am still getting stolen money from your area.

Definite proof of the gang we suspect. Only know one member – Billy Ferrell. Will forward Washington's reply with full details.

Yours sincerely,
Major Mart I. Campton

Clay folded the wire and shoved it into his pocket saying, "This is pretty good news from my uncle."

"How is Mart?"

"All right, I guess. Just rushes too much."

Mr. Phillips grinned. Clay could see the anxiety in the older man and gestured for him to take a chair. He then closed the office door and the door leading to the cells where his one prisoner, Billy Ferrell, was being kept.

"Well, since you've been away, things have really happened here."

Clay then explained everything to Mr. Phillips; from the morning he left until his return. He revealed how he had been beaten and dragged up the street with Pet's pleading for help and how Diamond had helped and why.

Then Clay said, "I told him he could stay at the hotel and that you'd give him a job at the ranch."

He explained the killing of Blair's men and the fact that Blair had wanted to hire Diamond on as a hired gun.

Mr. Phillips asked Clay, "Did they really put a pair of bloomers on you?"

"Damn it, yes. And I promised each one they'd eat a piece of them, and I mean to keep that promise."

Mr. Phillips laughed and Clay said, "I guess I was a sight at that!"

Clay finished his information to his friend and future partner by telling him how he had pinned the bull killing on Billy. He pointed, "That's the rifle over there."

Mr. Phillips walked over and examined the gun and said, "It would only take one shot from this cannon."

"I suppose you want the bull paid for?"

"Yeah, I've got a bill of sale for three hundred dollars. And, by the way, that Angus I got in Denver cost five hundred. Damn if things aren't going up."

"We're having a sort of court Monday over at the

Payday. You've got to be there. You want to talk to Billy?"

"What for? From what you've said, the man is guilty. But why kill the bull?"

Clay moved form his desk. "I'll tell you this, there's a lot tied up in this business and I figure Blair is behind it all. He's out after something big."

Clay never mentioned anything about the land grant to Mr. Phillips. He held it in reserve, waiting for the other reply from his uncle.

"Well, I guess the next thing is for you to meet Diamond."

"Since he's going to be working for me, I guess so."

Mr. Phillips walked over to the window and looked out. He heard Clay move. Not facing him, he inquired, "How's Pet been behaving? She ain't changed, has she?"

Clay took a little while to answer. "I'd say so, but you'll see."

Pet's father moved from the window, looking directly at Clay. The look asked Clay a question.

He grinned. "She's all right, sir."

"I think maybe she is at that, son. I just couldn't forgive you as a man unless you finished what you started. I was young once myself, you know."

Clay felt Mr. Phillips knew that he and Pet had been together, but wouldn't tell him unless he asked. He also knew the older man couldn't be sure of Pet's actions until he had seen her.

Mr. Phillips broke the chain of thought by saying, "Now that I've heard everything, I'm hungry. How about you? What say we get a bite to eat?"

"You go ahead. I'll wait till Old John comes back. He went up to the Graystones to get me a few things."

Clay walked to the porch with Mr. Phillips. Outside both men looked at the sky, which had begun to cloud up. The swift moving thunderheads, with their dark linings, shut out the sunlight as they passed.

Clay spoke. "Looks like rain."

"We need it. Look at the dust," replied Mr. Phillips. With a wave of his hand, he walked away towards the hotel.

Clay looked up the street and saw Old John toddling along. He waited until the old man got inside.

"Here we be, Marshal," quipped the old man, with a thin stream of tobacco juice flowing from the corner of his mouth.

"Just put that stuff over there and you can put the canned goods in the back room."

"Right, Marshal."

"I'll be gone for a while, so keep an eye on things, John."

"Will do, Marshal. Oh, I dang near forgot, that old buzzard Bryant told me to tell you to stop by the bank."

"Hmm. Wonder what he wants."

The old man switched his chew and wiped his seeping chin. "You the marshal, not me."

Clay left the office in a hurry. The sky was becoming darker and he wondered about his horse, Baldy. The big red was a bit nervous during storms. A stiffening breeze was beginning to blow, cooling the earth in its sweeping light touch. The breeze was a vigorous relief from the heat. The distant soft rolls of thunder sounded the approach of rain.

Inside the bank the clerk, a dried up little man with glasses riding the bridge of his nose, ushered Clay behind the cage to Mr. Bryant's office.

Mr. Bryant didn't offer a chair as he said, while standing himself; "I'll get right to the point, Marshal. We're forming a citizens committee, and we would be thankful for your cooperation. As a law officer, you have a duty to see to it that the wants of the people are carried out."

"Get to the point," Clay said. He could feel trouble brewing from the money hungry Mr. Bryant.

"It's this, Marshal. We feel the town would be better off without this nigger. If he stays around, he'll brings others, and we want our town to be for good white folks."

Clay's face reddened. He could see the injustice in the banker's remark.

"Listen, Bryant, he has just as much right to be here as you do, and as long as I'm the law, I'll protect his rights as well as yours."

Clay became angrier as he thought of the land grant and why this man, Bryant, hadn't mentioned it to him. Clay thought the man was hiding something, another good reason for him to be stirring up some sort of trouble.

"I thought you'd feel that way, Marshal. That's why I'm sending to Austin to the regional office and asking Major Campton to send a replacement."

"I take it you know Major Campton, then."

"Sure, I know him. And I don't like your actions in behalf of that nigger. The very idea of a white man, and a Marshal at that, siding with a nigger killer!"

With contempt Clay said, "You can withdraw my account from this bank, Bryant. I don't cotton to narrow-minded bankers."

He withdrew his money and watched as the banker

counted it out. "Bryant, that's the second mistake you've made." The banker stopped counting and looked up.

Clay didn't notice the few drops of rain that were beginning to come down faster. He hurried to the hotel, thinking about Bryant and his evil scheme. He couldn't put his finger on Bryant's reactions, yet he knew there was big trouble brewing and that Diamond, his friend, was being used as the scapegoat. He also knew the same trouble was aimed at him as well.

Mr. Phillips was sitting on the porch and, as Clay came up, he said, "That rain is a welcome relief, Clay."

"Yeah. Come up kind of quick."

"Here, Clay, take a chair before you eat; I've got something on my mind."

Before the two men could start talking, up walked Diamond himself, getting out of the rain. Mr. Phillips looked as the tall Negro approached. Clay waited and, with interest, noticed the intense attention Martin Phillips gave Diamond. Diamond, with a steady gaze, looked hard at Mr. Phillips in return. Clay could see concern in both men's eyes.

"Diamond, this here's Mr. Phillips, the man you'll be working for."

Clay was indeed glad that Diamond would be working out at the ranch. With him out of town, maybe things could cool down – for a while at least.

Diamond rubbed his hands on his pants as if cleaning them, but Clay saw the man was nervous. He smiled and said, "I'm real grateful, Mr. Phillips, for the job."

"That's all right. And is Diamond your real name?"

"Yes, it's Clifford Diamond, sir."

"I see," said Mr. Phillips and he flinched.

126

Clay noted that Mr. Phillips' actions were unusual. The man had a flushed face, was it embarrassment or dislike? Clay couldn't tell.

Then Mr. Phillip asked, "Where you from, Diamond?"

"Hell, he won't tell you that," said Clay.

Diamond paused as if thinking and said, "Down Texas way, but originally from New Orleans."

"Damn! He told you more in two questions than he's told me since he's been here," echoed Clay.

Diamond was still on edge, as was Mr. Phillips, making Clay feel uncomfortable.

"I'll be glad to have a good man around the ranch, Cliff, so you can move out there right after it stops raining. In fact, I'll ride out with you." To change the subject, he added, "Let's eat, men."

Clay prided himself on knowing men and their caliber, but couldn't figure out the distant, yet unexplained, actions of these two men. The three sat at the same table, not even mindful of the few harried looks thrown their way. The conversation was light, but each man was laboring to keep his it directed to the town itself. Clay, disgusted with all the pretense, said, "Maybe I'll ride out to the ranch with you two. I could use the exercise."

"Good, my boy, glad to have you," Mr. Phillips said. Then to Diamond he started, "Now, son…"

Diamond, dropped his fork. To cover, he arose from the table saying, "I'll be ready when you are."

He passed in front of Clay who looked up and could have sworn he saw hard tears in Diamond's eyes. Clay continued to watch the man as he walked up the stairs holding the butts of his guns as if fighting an impulse to use them.

Mr. Phillips caught Clay's eyes. They looked at one another.

Phillips said, "I think Cliff's got something on his mind."

"I guess you'd know, mister. If it's trouble, you'd better tell me about it."

"What makes you say that, Clay?"

"Have it your way, Martin. But I count you both as friends. I'd hate to believe either of you would try to deceive me."

"You got any ideas, Clay?"

"At least one. A man like Diamond don't cry for nothing, and it takes more than hate to shake him up."

"Clay, you know, you see too damned much!"

"You do know, then?"

"Yes and no."

"You may as well tell me, 'cause I already know he's here looking for a man. And judging from both of your reactions to each other, I'd say he's found him."

Clay offered Mr. Phillips a cigarette. Both men went back to the front porch to wait for Diamond. The rain was coming down in sheets, making riverlets in the muddy street. The wooden sidewalks, soaked to their fill, seemed to bulge. A fresh scent of hot earth mixed with animal scent was heavy. Clay looked out at the rain and relished the relief from the heat. Mr. Phillips looked through the rain into past years as if dreaming a dream of the damned.

FIFTEEN

The downpour let up after an hour. The sun re
turned, throwing heat waves that soaked up the
water from the earth. The three men, Marshal Clay
Clinton, Clifford Diamond. and Mr. Martin Phillips,
started their ride out to the dairy ranch, each man en-
grossed in his own thoughts. The mud from the horses'
hooves splattered fine flakes of mud upon the riders.
Clay was glad that Mr. Phillips was along. He knew he
had done the right thing by not mentioning his meeting with the banker, Mr. Bryant, to either Diamond or
Phillips. Clay would make it a point to discuss the
banker with Mr. Phillips once they got to the ranch.

Mr. Phillips occasionally stole glances at Diamond
as he rode, and his face would smile at an unseen pleasure. Mr. Phillips secretly admired the way his new
employee sat on his horse – tall, with his wide shoulders squared against the wind. Mr. Phillips lost all
sense of time in watching Diamond, but Clay figured
more was there than met the eye.

Diamond regained his stern composure and let the
ride relax him. He had done his looking at Mr. Phillips
from the hotel to the livery stable. Between that time

he had seen all he wished to see. He divined that once they got to the ranch, Mr. Phillips would talk to him. Here was to be the tested ties of a man in the presence of a man. Diamond knew the results of this meeting would be the reason for his staying in Pueblo or his reason for leaving.

All three men had the presence of mind that found the given task they all had to do, each a revelation to renew their faith in the good of all. Because the common foe of all three was, and had been, pressing, throwing a wall of hate from which, if they walked out, the acclaim would be everlasting victory.

The five-miles from town to the ranch hadn't taken long to cover. They dismounted in the yard.

Pet came from the house wearing a blue blouse, opened at the collar. Her father looked at her and saw with his own eyes what Mr. Graystone had meant.

Pet cried, "Dad, when did you get back?"

He laughed, handing her a small black case and said, "You must have known I'd have a present for you!"

Pet opened it excitedly, seeing the three strands of pearls. She gave them to Clay saying, "Here, put them on me!"

Clay was a bit stunned, but did as he was directed. Pet turned to Clay and kissed him.

Clay immediately looked at Mr. Phillips, who smiled and said, "Well, I see it's true."

Clay couldn't say a word. He felt like a thief, caught red-handed. Pet kissed her father and thanked him for the gift. Mr. Phillips could see in his daughter's face the look of a woman. She had grown up while he was gone. He again looked at Clay, in a way that seemed to say, "You rascal!"

Pet turned her head to Diamond, who looked on the happy greetings of his friend's woman. "Diamond, don't let my dad scare you. And, since you're here, maybe we'll get to know you better."

"That won't be hard to do, Miss Pet."

"I thought I told you my name is Pet. I like that," she stated.

Mr. Phillips was proud to show off the dairy ranch to Clay, he knew he'd make a good partner. Although Clay had been on the property before, he welcomed the chance to really see what he was going to be a part of. While the three men walked from place to place, Pet sat on the porch, quite content just watching. Mr. Phillips showed Clay the springhouse where the milk was strained and canned, plus the vat where the milk and cheese was made. He took pleasure in cutting the cheese he made and offering each a piece. Their comments were more than pleasing.

Diamond examined the butter churn, evidently liking what he saw. Mr. Phillips pointed out the bullpen where the new bull would be kept. They entered the cow barn where the evening milking was being done by the seven men Mr. Phillips had working for him. Each looked at the men as they passed, giving special notice to Diamond and his guns.

They toured the area, with Mr. Phillips telling them both how he wanted to expand and how the summer was rough on the products without ice.

Diamond asked him, "Why don't you cut ice from the river in the winter and store it for use in the summer?"

Mr. Phillips and Clay were surprised at the man's foresight. "Damned good idea," exclaimed Mr. Phillips.

Clay added, "Diamond, with such good ideas, this

place is a gold mine."

Seeing that Mr. Phillips was well pleased with a solution to one of his problems, the men stood around talking until after the milking was done. The workmen came from the barn carrying pails of milk.

Mr. Phillips called out, "Harvey, come over here for a minute!"

"What you want, Mr. Phillips?" asked the man.

"Take Cliff here and show him to the boys' bunkhouse. He'll be with us for a while."

Without a word, the middle-aged man called Harvey led Diamond away.

Mr. Phillips and Clay started towards the house when another one of the men called out, "Hey, Mr. Phillips. Just a second!"

They waited until the man, who had a red face, was about in his late twenties with beady eyes and a heavy set of shoulders, stood facing them.

"Listen, Pet just told us you hired a nigger!" he said.

"What about it, Sandy?"

"What about it? You don't expect us to sleep in the same bunkhouse with a nigger, do you?"

Mr. Phillips hadn't given this any thought before, but said calmly, "One man working for me is as good as any other, Sandy." He continued, "A man's color don't make him no less a man."

"Well, you can find yourself another hand. I don't figure to sleep nowhere near a nigger."

Mr. Phillips withdrew some money from his pocket. "Here's your money, Sandy. Sorry you feel that way. Just clear out."

Taking his pay, Sandy remarked, "I'll do that. Right now!"

Clay could see the hurt on Mr. Phillips' face. Seeing Pet, he knew she'd heard the remarks as well.

"It's a shame, Clay, but I never figured people could hate so much without any reason."

"Perhaps you're better off without him."

"Maybe so, Clay, maybe so."

Diamond appeared and Mr. Phillips called, "Cliff, come on up to the house for a while."

Then he turned back to Clay, but Clay said, "I got to be riding back to town."

"Me too!" echoed Pet, her voice excited.

"You two go ahead, I'll ride in later. I want to talk to Diamond."

Clay looked at Diamond and said, "You gonna be all right?"

Diamond understood Clay's look and put forth his hand. When Clay's hand clasped his, he reassured his friend, "Everything's going to be fine, Clay. There won't be no trouble."

Diamond watched Pet and Clay as they rode off back towards town.

"Come on in," ordered Mr. Phillips, leading the way into a large parlor furnished with good homemade furniture, complimented with a stuffed horsehair sofa and extra chairs with bold patterned Indian blankets. Pet had made all the tapestries and woven rugs for the floor. The big five-room, cabin-type house was well constructed, and clearly showed a woman's touch. It was immaculately clean.

Mr. Phillips stood in front of the open fireplace, gesturing for the Negro to take a seat. The elder man, with his white hair and heavy mustache adding a quiet distinction to his person, said, "I guess you have a lot on your mind, Cliff."

"Not too much. I'm more curious than anything else. It all depends on you."

"Yes, I guess it does. Frankly, Cliff, I figured I'd never see you again."

"Maybe you did. But the point is, did you ever want to?"

Mr. Phillips jammed both hands into his pockets. "Yes, Cliff, I did. I've always wanted to see you as a man. And, now that I have, I wonder."

Diamonds words came slow and even. "Do you know why I'm here?"

"No, but I can guess."

"You might guess, but I doubt if you know." Diamond was straining to keep himself from blurting out his feelings.

"Tell me, Clifford, how did you know that I was in Pueblo?"

"I didn't. But two years after you left, right before Ma died, she asked me to find you and forgive you."

Diamond withdrew a picture from his pocket. "Here, she wanted you to have this."

Mr. Phillips took the picture in the embossed golden locket. He looked at it with tenderness. The past years seemed to make him smile as he remembered and recalled to mind Diamond's mother, a beautiful mulatto; his wife, to whom he'd been secretly married.

At the time he was a young doctor in his late twenties. He had loved Sarah Lee Phillips with a deep appreciation for her as a woman. During that time, it was a credit to have a Negro mistress; but young Dr. Phillips went a step further – he married the woman he loved.

When the bouncing baby boy was born, Mr. Phillips

remembered his Negro wife saying, "See the jewel I've given you?" Thus he was christened Clifford Diamond Phillips.

For ten years he had watched Diamond grow. He was a fine, strong boy of ten, with wavy black hair, clear, blue-black eyes, and a keen jaw taken from his father.

Again he recalled to mind his wife's remark, "Indeed, Martin, your son has you in his blood. You'll always see yourself in him." That had been twenty-five years ago.

Then trouble came. The governor's son and his companion, in a drunken state, had ripped the clothes from his wife's body and used her for their sporting pleasure. The doctor had just ridden in from a call when he heard his wife's screams. Seeing the man, half naked on top of the love of his life, he flew into a rage. Taking the pistol he carried in his bag for emergencies, he shot him several times in the back. He hadn't even noticed the man's companion, who ran back to the governor to tell him his son had been shot.

Shocked that he'd been able to take another man's life, and seeing no other way out, Dr. Phillips left Sarah Lee and his son. He fled from Texas into Mexico, where he lost all identity as Dr. Phillips, leaving behind the wife and son he had loved.

Mr. Phillips' eyes were moist as he looked upon his son, not caring if he was black or white, but wondering what a father could do to make it all up to the son he'd left at the hands of mercy.

Diamond could see his father was a hurt man and that his sorrow was genuine. He related how the governor had had him and his mother jailed for two years. When his mother died, her last wish was for him to see his father and forgive him as she had done. The picture was the only worldly possession his mother had, and she'd sent that to her husband.

Mr. Phillips could tell Diamond knew the truth from his mother, yet he felt he had to tell him himself. He revealed the story in detail to his son.

After he finished, he asked, "Tell me, son, what can a father do or say to his boy after all these years?"

"I don't know, sir, but my biggest worry was if you would even acknowledge me as your son or a ..."

"Why, boy," said Mr. Phillips, "why shouldn't I? You are my flesh and blood, you and Pet."

Diamond looked at his father, knowing that Pet did not know.

"Pet! My God! A man with two children, one white and one black."

Diamond continued to watch him. Then his father said, "Damned the place that makes a difference!"

Diamond couldn't bring himself to answer or make a remark just then, but later on he spoke in a cultivated tone, "I've often wanted to remember my Pa and to be a doctor just like him. As a young boy, when I last remembered you, I could never understand why my pa had to leave. Ma explained it to me by saying, 'When the time comes he'll either come back or send for you.' I came to the conclusion in later years that you just didn't want me around you; but now I'm sorry, for I see you couldn't come back."

Both men were silent. Diamond walked over to the window and looked out.

"How will you tell your daughter about me?"

"I hadn't intended to tell her."

The son turned from the window. "Don't you think

she has a right to know? She's no child, but a woman who's old enough to understand."

His father agreed. "Yes! Yes, she should know. I'll see to it. Now tell me, son, you're going to stay, aren't you?"

Mr. Phillips was anxious to keep his son around, but was a bit fearful.

"For a while I'll be around, and then I'll be going out California way."

This saddened the old man, but he knew Cliff was trying to make things easier for him and he was grateful for that.

Diamond returned to the barn, feeling an elated joy mixed with pain and confusion, remembering his father's last words, "Remember, son, you're working for me as a son. I'll make it up to you, what I can. Don't ever forget that you are a man with a job to do, but above all, you are my son. I'm sorry there's no fatted calf, but still, you have the rights of a son, not a workman."

SIXTEEN

Monday morning burst forth with the sun, the day of Billy Ferrell's trial.

The towns people all crowded into the makeshift courtroom of Kate's Payday Casino. Chairs were not enough; the standing room took every inch. Windows were opened where men stood in the depth of two's looking in. Some folks came just out of mere curiosity, while others were really interested in the proceedings. The twelve men of the jury were selected at random. Because of the great respect most of them had for Mr. Graystone he was given the job of judging or sitting to rule.

Blair Tyson and his boys were in evidence, but it was obvious that Marshal Clay Clinton's orders about wearing guns were being carried out. Behind Kate's bar the men's guns hung on pegs by the mirror.

Billy Ferrell sat at a table alone with Blair, who, naturally, was acting as his lawyer.

Men who had some interest in business were present and even a few women were gathered around to witness the new law in town.

When the proceeding started, Kate took place at

the corner of the piano, her eyes on Clay.

Mr. Graystone, seated at another table, called the court to order. Clay presented his case, showing the judge and the jury the evidence.

Blair Tyson listened but made no outcry.

The judge asked Mr. Phillips, "Since the bull was your property, what do you think should be done?"

"I want to be reimbursed for the cost of my bull. Here's the original bill of sale for three hundred dollars."

Blair Tyson arose from his chair stating, "Mr. Graystone, my client admits he was drunk and mistook the bull for a wild black bear, so we are prepared to pay the fine."

The court roared with laughter and had to be quieted down with a few raps of the judge's gavel.

Clay was surprised at the fast turn of events. He knew the man meant no good, but was powerless to do anything until he knew what was afoot.

However, when Blair paid the fine for Billy, Clay stepped up and in a loud voice said, "Blair, don't forget to add a hundred dollars for trespassing and predatory slaying. You see, we need a little money to build a courthouse."

Blair paused and heard Mr. Graystone say, "Fine, one hundred dollars."

Mr. Graystone received the money and wrote a receipt for Blair to sign, called Mr. Phillips to the table and paid him the three hundred dollars for the bull Billy had killed.

Then Clay said, "You can go now, Billy, but I've still got an eye on you."

Billy left his chair and elbowed his way to where Texas Red Morgan was standing.

Clay thought the court session was over until he heard Blair say, "Gentlemen, now that the matter of the Phillips' bull is over, we have another matter to discuss." He turned to Clay who was talking to Kate and Mr. Phillips. "This will concern you and Phillips, Marshal."

Tension began to fill the room. Blair continued. "Since most of you people here own businesses which the town needs, you can see the need for and agree to our citizens committee, which Mr. Bryant can explain to you in detail."

Clay, with a leering smile on his face, knew what was coming, and his hatred for the banker grew.

The banker, Clark Bryant, addressed the group. "Ladies and gentlemen; as the sponsor and head of the citizens committee, we have a big black problem on our hands which the marshal would rather overlook."

"What's he talking about, Clay?" asked Mr. Phillips.

"This is about your new worker," said the banker as he tugged at his gravy-stained vest and added, "Not only that, but the Phillips hotel lets this black stay there and eat there! Now that's Phillips' business, but when a black man kills two men, it's time somebody took a hand."

Billy cut right in on the banker's speech by shouting, "We got a marshal now, and we of the citizens committee want him to either run this nigger out of town or arrest him for the murder of those two men. And, since we're law-abiding citizens, it's up to us to see that the marshal does his duty. Remember, he didn't hesitate to lock up a white man for accidentally shooting a bull. Now let's see him do his duty to this nigger. Or do we take matters into our own hands?"

Mr. Phillips knew that this was a threat of mob rule, and could not help but try to think of a way to help his son. He wanted to tell the whole room that Diamond was his son, but he just couldn't. He could only, at this moment, depend on Clay for a defense.

Clay's anger was mounting. He could plainly see that Blair was behind getting rid of Diamond because he was afraid of the man. And it was a plot to get rid of him as marshal at the same time. He had to stall. He knew Blair had been holding his men off for a reason but he didn't think that this was it. Clay had to find the connection between the banker, Clark Bryant and Blair Tyson.

The marshal turned and addressed his remarks to both men hotly, "Get this through your thick skulls. As long as I'm Marshal, no man goes to jail for killing another in self-defense. You, Blair, you egged your hounds on Diamond and got them killed. You're taking a big step towards hell if you bother Diamond without reason."

Then, he added, by way of catching Blair by the shirt, "I've already got good reason to kill you, so don't push your luck." He pushed Blair backward with a shove. "And you, Bryant, you'd better get yourself in order, 'cause I'll be seeing you!"

Blair and Bryant took the affront without a word. Nothing Clay did would cause them to show their hands. The meeting broke up with Kate doing business as usual. Mr. Phillips left with Clay and Mr. Graystone. Texas Red Morgan led the gang members to Blair's office where they had another discussion.

Blair was seething with rage and said, "Just as soon as the big job is done, we're killing that nigger and that

141

son of a bitch marshal."

"Hell, Blair, they don't suspect nothing. Why don't we just get 'em now?"

"Damn you, Billy. Don't you know if we killed that nigger we'd have to kill the marshal? Then every lawman and ranger from Texas would be here. Just wait. Remember, I'm anxious to get them both myself."

With their chests cleared, they made further plans for the train robbery, which was only a few days away. Blair had set the robbery for the first of July, after changing his plans about the Phillips' dairy ranch.

The marshal, Mr. Phillips and Mr. Graystone all entered the general store. Mr. Phillips showed more concern than anyone.

Mr. Graystone was the first to speak. "Seems to me, Martin, Bryant is a little too fast in forming a committee."

"You let me handle Bryant," remarked Clay. Clay, forming a plan of action in his mind, asked the storeowner, "Do you have any money in Bryant's bank, Mr. Graystone?"

"Yep, I've got a few dollars. Why?" Clay's plan was a bold one, but he thought it might lead to something.

"Go and draw out every penny and give it to me for safe keeping."

"You wait a minute, Marshal. It ain't that I don't trust you, but every cent I've got is in that bank."

"Go ahead, Elmer," said Mr. Phillips. "I'll do the same. Whatever the marshal has in mind, I'll go along with his plan."

"My plan is to make Mr. Bryant think there's going to be a run on the bank, enough to make him show his hand."

"Sounds good," answered Graystone, "but suppose nothing happens."

"Just leave it to me," replied Clay. After Mr. Graystone agreed, along with Mr. Phillips, the plan was considered in effect.

Clay and Mr. Phillips walked over to the railroad station, where Clay sent another wire to his uncle.

Returning back to the center of town, Clay asked Mr. Phillips, "Do you think you can keep Diamond on the ranch?"

"Clay, you know as well as I do that he'll hear about all this and..."

"No! I don't want him to know."

"How are you going to keep him from knowing?"

Clay thought it over and replied, "That's all right, I'll tell him. It might be better for him to know."

"I agree."

Clay took a few more steps and asked, "Did everything go well after Pet and I left?"

Mr. Phillips knew well what he meant and answered honestly, "Yes, quite well. In fact, I find Diamond quite a man."

Clay laughed. "You'd be a poor excuse for kinfolks if you didn't"

Mr. Phillips betrayed his own confidence and started at Clay. "What kinfolks?"

Clay confessed. "When a man like Diamond lets something unnerve him, it's one of two things, his family or a woman. Had he wanted to kill you, he would have. But when you called him 'son' at the table, he had tears in his eyes so I just put two and two together and got a perfect score.

"Damn you, Clay. You always see too much. I guess

I might as well tell you. Diamond..."

"You don't have to tell me, Martin. I figured he was your boy. Just look at his eyes and his face and you can see it. But the big question I've got is, are you going to tell Pet?"

Mr. Phillips breathed heavily. "I will tell her, but not yet. And while we're at it, I want to ask you a question. Do you intend to do right by Pet?"

"Do right? What do you mean by that?" Clay was on the defensive.

"I hope your weren't just sowing wild oats while I was in Denver."

Clay couldn't get around Mr. Phillips so he answered, "I intend to marry her, if that's what you mean."

"That's what I mean. So I won't worry about it anymore. Now the problem is Pet and her half brother."

"Yeah, it's a problem," said Clay.

"How do you feel about Diamond as kin, Clay?"

"I never thought about it. I ain't marrying Diamond."

"I see," agreed the old man.

When they reached the hotel Clay and his friend departed with Mr. Phillips saying, "I expect the bull to arrive on the first of the month."

"Good!" waved Clay.

Riding herd on a town like Pueblo, Clay stayed busy for the rest of the day. He visited shops and saw that people were in a healthy state of mind.

Later in the afternoon he rode out to the Bryant spread to have a look around. On his way back he saw a cloud of dust far down the trail approaching him. He didn't wish to meet anyone on the road leading to the

Bryant ranch, so he rode into a thicket of pinion and pine, where he led Baldy a few feet further into the wooded area and ground-tied him. Then he walked back to see who was riding the ranch road.

Within a few minutes the riders approached. Clay recognized Blair Tyson and the banker, Clark Bryant. The men rode on at a fast trot, leaving a wake of dust. From where Clay stood, he overheard the statement, "Kill them!" From another he heard, "...job to be done..."

The overheard remarks caused Clay's mind to concentrate. He couldn't figure their connection. But the presence of Blair and the banker riding together meant that they were indeed connected in some way and he had to find out how.

On his way back to Pueblo, Clay mulled over the scene, including Diamond. He had six or seven pieces to the puzzle and none fit; yet he was pleased to know about Blair and Bryant's secret meeting. He understood the citizens committee business and divined that if Blair had Bryant in that much of a grip then Bryant knew more about Blair's operation than anybody. Clay toyed with the idea of Blair and Bryant being partners in the bank with Blair holding a lesser share. He was convinced now more than ever that having Graystone and Phillips draw their money from the bank would cause a stir.

When Clay got back to town he left Baldy at the livery stable and went directly to his office at the jail. He exchanged a few words with Old John and watched the old man shuffle off, going to get something to eat.

Two things happened while he was at the jail. Mr. Graystone brought him five thousand dollars, the money he'd withdrawn from the bank. Then Kate came over to the jail. They talked mostly of Pet until Kate said, "Clay, how many men can you count on in this town?"

His eyebrows arched in surprise. "Frankly, Kate, no one. I'm just a lone marshal."

"What about the nigger?"

"What about him, Kate?"

"Can you depend on him if any trouble starts?"

"What makes you think there will be trouble?"

"Hell, Clay, I heard the talk in court and more afterwards, and I saw Blair and Bryant ride out together. Course, that don't mean anything. But later this afternoon, while you were out, Graystone and Phillips both withdrew their money from the bank."

"It's their money," said Clay, looking unconcerned.

"Yeah, but if they draw out their money, it's for a good reason. And, just to be safe, I'm going to do the same. I don't think the bank can stand a run on it."

Clay was more than satisfied, but told Kate, "No, you keep your money in the bank. But you can do me a favor."

"Just ask it... I hope it's something only a woman can do," Kate said slyly.

Clay laughed at her pointed suggestion, but said seriously, "Here, take this money. There's five thousand dollars there. Put it in the bank tomorrow, then write a check payable to Phillips for two thousand dollars. You understand?"

"Yeah, gut..."

"No buts. Just do as I say."

"All right, you win, Clay. Now, how's your social life going?"

"Not bad, Kate. I just might become real sociable like."

"Not after that sweet fruit deal," she laughed.

Kate had stayed for about a half an hour. After she left, Clay had his plans well in progress. When Old John returned, he decided it was time for some supper.

He again checked over everything in his mind and ran a fix on the next problem he had to bring into view; that of Diamond and his family, especially Pet.

SEVENTEEN

It was a few days later when Diamond, after finishing his work, got on his horse and headed for town. Since the day was still light, he ambled along, not caring too much about anything. His foremost thoughts were taken up with his family problems. Getting to know Pet, his half sister, he almost began to worship her. No one had told him what was being said about him in town. And he knew who he was, a Negro with a white father!

Diamond realized that his coming to Pueblo, and especially his staying in Pueblo, didn't set too well with some of the citizens. These things were laying dominant in his mind.

As for Marshal Clay Clinton, Diamond knew him to be fair and impartial. His biggest worry was not to cause a showdown in town with the members of Blair Tyson's gang, including Blair himself. Diamond knew trouble was to be expected, but didn't know when or what form it would take. He also realized that his friendship with the marshal wasn't particularly liked, yet Clay had been a man and Diamond appreciated this. Even the job with his father was proof that both his father and the marshal had his best interests at heart. All these things came rushing forward in his mind, together with the thought that he would have a talk with Clay while in town.

Diamond, riding his big blue roan, came out of the trail road into a wooded section of the ranch. The sun was just beginning to go down under cover of the coming night, with shadows hiding and dancing in little niches, making him alert. The country was beautiful, and everywhere he looked gave him a sense of appreciation, though his travels had been too many and too far. Here in the Colorado basin was the Promised Land, offering a man great returns for his labor.

Diamond stopped to rest his horse and smoke one of the cigarettes Clay had given him. He looked at the far distant blue Pike's Peak, the azure splendor of nature's painting with a hidden brush, the lively tones of the earth, the sky and the trees. Looking back towards his father's ranch, he could see the rooftops of buildings and white fences. He spurred his big roan into motion again.

Diamond was a little less than halfway to town on the rocky edge of a coulee when the big blue roan snorted and neighed. On the hard lava rock, Diamond checked the horse, and his keen eyes sighted the cause of the horse's skittish actions. About three feet away a large timber rattler had been disturbed and was now in the process of coiling to deal its warning rattle. A quick shot from one of his guns put him and his horse at ease, blowing the head clear off the snake's body. Diamond comforted the big roan by patting its neck and gently reassuring him.

No sooner than the horse had quieted down, a

piercing scream rang through the air. The horse's ears became pinpoints of warning. Diamond's sense of caution turned towards the scream. It was a woman's voice and instantly he thought of Pet, even though he had left her at the ranch.

With haste, he urged the animal towards the scream coming from the left. He rounded a large boulder that hid the curve in the trail and saw a saddled horse prancing but being held by somebody on the ground. Dismounting with one gun drawn, he approached and saw the crying woman thrashing about on the grassy side of the road. Diamond immediately saw the light movement of the grass and reached it, stomping his foot and feeling the softness of the snake's flesh give way to a messy pulp.

Kate, still crying and frightened after being thrown from her horse, met Diamond's eyes.

He asked, "Did he bite you?"

She said haltingly, "I don't know." She let the reins slip from her hand and moaned, "Oh, my leg."

Diamond, kneeling beside her, remarked, "Here, let me see. Where does it hurt?"

She hesitated. Diamond reached for her petticoat; she withdrew from his touch. He looked at her in dismay, feeling her indignation and resentment at his touching her.

He said angrily, "Look, Kate, this is not the time to stand on your virtue and your ideas of morality and righteous dignity. Whether you know it or not, your life is involved."

She heard him clearly and understood perfectly. She then, without ceremony, raised her skirt, exposing her upper thigh where the white flesh was puffy and swelling with an angry red. She and Diamond saw the two neatly placed punctures made by the rattler's fangs.

"This may hurt, so hold on!"

He expertly sliced her thigh between the two fang marks, causing a rivulet of bluish blood to flow. Diamond saw that the blood wasn't clear red. He looked at Kate, who only squirmed from the rapid lancing.

He then pressed his mouth hard to the wound to form a suction for a few minutes. When he stopped, he saw the color of the blood was bright, indicating there was no poison left.

Without looking at Kate, he removed the lead from one of his bullets and poured the black powder into the open flesh.

"Jesus, that stings like hell!" she exclaimed.

He didn't answer, but finished the work on the wound and, by cutting strips from her petticoat, carefully bandaged her thigh.

As Diamond had worked to save her life, Kate could feel his hands on her body. She half interpreted them in a lustful way, but her good reason said it was necessary. She felt strangely queer when he drew the poisoned blood from her body with his mouth. She pictured his lips on other parts of her body. Her thoughts were a mixture of thankfulness and reproach. Yet she knew he had saved her life.

He helped her up. She stood leaning against him.

With emotion Diamond said, "I think we're nearer to the ranch than to town; you'd better stay there tonight."

Kate had a bit of pity in her eyes and just nodded her head in agreement.

He helped her to her horse, easily lifting her body. She felt the strong muscles come into work as the tips of his fingers accidentally brushed across her breasts. For support, she placed one arm around her rescuer's neck. He placed her on the animal's back.

Standing beside the horse as he gave her the reins, he said, "I'll ride beside you in case you feel weak."

Kate rode beside the Negro, realizing that what she had told Pet was the truth. Even LeeLee knew. But she was determined to fight it.

The sun was all but gone now and a wonder-like quietness filled the air. Birds flew to nests without chirps. Only the sound of the ruffled hooves of their horses in the grassy road could be heard, along with a few night creatures out in search of food.

Kate stole glances at the tall, well-built man riding beside her close enough to catch her if she did feel faint. She was angry with herself for the feeling, but still hated him. She could still see and feel his hands upon her thigh. She resented this. At least she told herself she did, knowing now she wanted him more than ever.

During the slow trip back to the ranch, there were no attempts at conversation. When they reached the ranch, the house was dark. Only a light from the bunkhouse said anyone was around.

Diamond stepped from his saddle and helped Kate down. "I can walk, I think," she said.

"Better not. If there's more poison in that bite you don't want to circulate it."

He then picked her up. Again, his fingers touched her breasts. This time she was overcome with a true feeling for the man and sighed, "Oh, Diamond."

He looked at her and saw that she was relaxed. She

had passed out.

He carried her into the house and through the parlor to a bedroom, where he placed her gently upon the bed. He really looked at her for the first time as a woman. A nervousness shot through him, telling him his feelings were becoming more than casual for this woman. Finding a lamp, he located a bottle of whiskey. He brought it back to the bedroom and forced a bit of it down Kate's throat. She coughed and sprayed the whiskey all over herself and him. After she'd gotten her breath, he propped her up in bed, putting a pillow behind her back.

He went out and brought some milk to her and said, "Better drink this until you get your strength back."

Kate couldn't take her eyes from him, now that the closeness of his body and hands had delayed effect on her. She had begun to see the Negro as a man, void of color. Whether he was black or white made no difference to her now. She reflected on how many men wouldn't have done what he did. She could see and feel his strong arms about her, yet she felt he was as tender as a child. After a long pause she said, "Thanks."

"Pet must have taken the back road to town. I'll get one of the men to ride in and get her to stay with you. Is there anything else you want?"

"No. Just ask him to tell LeeLee to look after things until I get back."

Diamond returned after asking one of the men to make the errand. In the meantime, he stabled the horses.

When he entered the room, Kate had raised her skirt and was looking at the bandage. For some reason, she didn't even try to hide her thighs from his view.

She saw the effect the exposed thigh was having on him by the bulge beginning to form in his pants.

She said, "Come over here a second and sit down." Her hand patted the side of the bed where she wanted him to sit.

Diamond came and sat down, looking at her.

"Tell me," she asked, "Why don't you stay with me? You afraid I'll bite?"

He smiled. "With people around here, Kate, it's already hard enough. You understand that!"

"Sure. It's a problem, I know, but tell me, Diamond, when you came into the payday... Listen, what I really want to know is... What's here that you want?"

"I found what I came for, Kate."

"Oh. And you're telling me it's none of my business."

"No, I'm not, but..."

She cut him off. "Was it a woman you came for?"

Diamond realized she was referring to Madam LaCall's maid. "No, Kate, it wasn't a woman. I can always buy a woman. I was looking for a friend."

"Are you telling me you aren't interested in women in this back country?"

He smiled again. "Kate, what's on your mind?"

She frowned at his point blank question. "Well, when I saw you around the Payday I thought you wanted a woman. After all, every man needs a woman at some time you know."

"That's true, Kate, but the woman I have must also be a friend, if you know what I mean."

"I do."

"Kate, can I ask you a frank question?"

"Go ahead. There's very little of me you haven't seen, so we know each other by now."

Her remark was pointed and she saw the bulge in his pants get larger.

He tinged and dropped his eyes. "What I want to know is why you hate me so. I could tell it the second time I saw you, if not the first time."

"Don't you know?"

"No, I don't know. That's why I'm asking."

Kate knew then his experiences with women were limited and he really didn't know.

"I hated you for the reason any woman hates a man who doesn't pay attention to her."

His face lit up, revealing his surprise. "But, Kate, I..."

She interrupted by saying, "Yes, I know you didn't have me on your mind, but I had you on mine. I wanted to attract your attention so you would look at me possessively and I could tease you and laugh at you for wanting me."

She took his hand and continued, "But, Diamond, it didn't work like that at all. You paid me no mind, and my hate turned into something bigger."

He knew what she was telling him and asked, "But why me, Kate? A white man can give you more, and what can I offer you but trouble?"

"I thought of that, too, Cliff, and I found the answer tonight. You can give me yourself. That's all a woman needs from a man."

Kate then brought his hand up and held it to her breasts, at the same time reaching to him. He trembled from the shock. She knew it to be his innocence of her kind of woman, and she knew, too, that she'd gotten beyond his defenses.

Kate raised her lips to be kissed. She knew he was timid and afraid of her. She comforted him by saying,

"Not tonight, my darling, I want you all to myself. There's plenty of time for us to make love completely. Will you promise to come and see me soon at the Payday?"

Diamond could only nod.

Kate smiled and said, "I'm just a woman. Can't you see?"

Again she placed his hand upon her breast and squeezed it. As his hand trembled, he followed her lead.

"Diamond," she breathed, "I'm too weak now, but soon – very soon! They say the rarest pearl is black, darling, so is mine – a black jewel – a black diamond is so rare!"

EIGHTEEN

The sound of hooves in the yard and footsteps on the porch caused Diamond's release of Kate. Diamond was standing when Pet entered.

Seeing Diamond standing by, she asked, "Well, Kate, what happened?"

"A damned rattler got me!"

Pet mischievously smiled and said, "What kind, a black one?"

Kate flushed at the implication and told Pet what had happened.

Then Diamond said, "I sent for you 'cause she'll probably have chills and a high fever and will need somebody around for a day or two."

Pet remained calm, surveying the situation.

"Well, Kate, the next thing for you is rest," Diamond told her. He looked at Pet and said, "I'll be going. And thanks for coming, Pet."

"If we need you I'll call," answered Pet.

"Thanks again, Cliff," called Kate.

He waved his hand and left the room to the women. After Kate had changed into some of Pet's nightclothes and was in bed, Pet changed herself and decided to sit up with Kate. The chatted for a while.

When Kate began to feel the effects of the bite, she became feverish. Pet applied cold compresses throughout the night. Kate got along pretty good with Pet's help.

During the next day Kate stayed in bed. Diamond found no reason or excuse to come near the house. Pet went about her daily work, stopping every so often to look in on Kate. Late that evening Clay and Mr. Phillips rode in and called Diamond up to the house.

Mr. Phillips, Clay and Diamond went in to see how Kate was feeling. They found her in good spirits. Clay made everyone laugh when he said; "It takes more than a rattler to put Kate out of business!"

Kate looked at Diamond with thoughtful eyes and said, "But think, if Cliff hadn't come along, I'd really be out of business."

"You sure you didn't plan it that way?" echoed Pet.

Pet's remark went unanswered.

Resigned stares were directed at Kate, who quipped with a witty remark, "I wish I had been that wise. At least never underestimate a woman." Their faces broke into smiles.

Mr. Phillips said, "Well, we men have got a few things to talk about. We'll see you women later."

The three men took seats in the front parlor, with Clay doing all the talking.

"Cliff, we rode out here mainly to see you."

"What's on your mind, Clay?"

"Frankly, we've got a proposition for you. Me and your fa – I mean, Mr. Phillips, have talked this thing out fairly well, but you've got to know the score."

Diamond looked at Clay, then back at his father

before he spoke, "Let's hear it."

"I'm the marshal of Pueblo, that's true, but certain things I can't control or even do anything about until after they happen."

Mr. Phillips looked stranded, but said, "Son, what Clay is saying is…" He stopped.

Clay finished the statement. "Cliff, all hell is going to bust around Pueblo pretty soon and it concerns you most of all."

Diamond knew what he meant; the dirty business of being black from birth hadn't been forgotten.

Mr. Phillips spoke, "Now mind you, boy, it isn't the town people, but some of them can be led. It's Blair and his mob that's really after you."

"That's what I figured. I guess you came to ask me to leave town – run out of Pueblo for my own good! Is that it?" He looked at Clay.

"Partly, but I know you won't. So, there ain't nothing we can do unless we run you out, but then you'll only come back."

Diamond laughed, looked at his father, then asked, "What's your idea?"

"I don't want no mob killing my son!"

He had, in that moment of excitement revealed what Clay already knew.

Diamond looked sternly at Clay. He answered his father by saying, "I understand your point, but, hell, I can't keep running from my color for the rest of my life."

He felt proud that his father had acknowledged him as his son in front of Clay and added, "I was put in jail once by a mob when I was a child, and I'll die and go to hell before I go to jail again, mob or no mob!"

Seeing the man was upset, Clay said, "Hold on. We only thought we'd tell you the score, then let you decide."

"Well, I've decided. And hear me out. I'm not on the side of the law 'cause it stinks like hell, but Clay, in this I'll side with you and my Pa against Blair. Other than that, I'll fight my own battles."

"I appreciate that, Cliff, and I figured you would. But let me warn you. Not only are they out to nail you but me as well. One thing's for sure, as long as I'm the law any man that needs to be jailed will be."

Diamond knew that he meant what he said. But he had meant what he'd said, too.

"I don't expect we'll ever come to that, Clay."

"Let's hope not," replied Clay.

Mr. Phillips felt the load of the conversation upon him and began to unload by saying, "I never expected you to run away, so all we can do now is to tell you everything that is going on. That way you won't be caught off guard."

Clay took up the conversation and explained everything to Diamond, right down to Kate taking Greystone's money and writing a check payable to his father. Diamond learned that the check had been cashed and the money was paid in gold, as Clay had wanted it.

This was how they'd learned all the money from the check had been stolen, also that the bank was a blind to keep money in circulation in Pueblo and points west.

The baffling problem was still discovering who was behind it all? It was a clever master scheme.

Clay revealed everything except the land grant. This was his tie rope for the whole operation.

The personal scores to be settled were laid aside, but Diamond and Clay both knew, from what was revealed and talked about, that the personal scores couldn't be separated; it was tied with bringing Blair and his gang to justice.

Diamond told Clay, "From what's been said here tonight, I guess you know about me and all?"

"I half suspected it. You don't have to look too close to see the truth."

Mr. Phillips sighed with relief.

Diamond asked, "Does this make any difference? Or do you think you owe something?"

Clay became angered and said coldly, "What a man is, is of no concern to me, unless he makes it so. I've never been on any social terms with a Negro; but in your case exception is the rule. I like you as a man, and I feel, since I know you, my back can be safe. Don't many white men offer that. This is new for me, and I'm bound to make mistakes. Just be the man you are and don't hold them against me."

Here was a welcome sight as the two younger men, one white and the other black, clasped hands for the second time, in agreement of each being human beings with their backs together fighting for a cause. Each for his own reason, but still a common goal.

***

Meanwhile, back in town that same night, Blair Tyson came out on the street. He had seen the rider come for Pet, and wondered what could have happened out at the dairy ranch. He walked up the street, stopping at the shop of Madam LaCall. He looked up and down the street, inserted a key in the shop door and turned the latch. As usual, he undressed and slid into bed beside the form already there. He paid no particular attention to the woman already in the bed. She'd always been there waiting, never knowing when Mr. Blair would come but knowing he would.

Blair put his hands on the woman's body and felt the strange sensations of manly urges. He whispered into the woman's ear, "Hey, Emma, my black beauty, aren't you going to love me?"

The woman turned to him, as her hand toyed with him.

"Ah, that feels good," Blair sighed.

"It should."

The voice was strange, and he raised himself up saying, "Emma, damned if you don't sound like Madam LaCall!"

A sly, gleeful laugh came from the woman, then she spoke, "It should because I am Madam LaCall."

The surprise struck Blair like a bullet. Trapped, caught, he thought of trying to ease his way out of bed.

"No, no, my Cherie. If you don't stay I think quite a few people would like to know you sleep with my Negro maid."

This made Blair stop. "But I... I..."

"I nothing, you young scamp. I've suspected this for quite some time. That's why I sent Emma to Denver for a few days."

Still astounded, Blair asked, "But why?"

Madam LaCall laughed. "But why? So I could take her place. I'm French, you know."

"You didn't have to go to all this trouble," chuckled Blair.

"No, but it's much better this way. The game, the sport of trapping you, young man. Now let's you and I do what you came for!"

Not that Madam LaCall wasn't desirable to some men, but not to Blair. He tried to get himself in the mood for her but couldn't do it, and said with a wry smile, "You'd better help me overcome the surprise."

"That's quite easy for a French woman, now that I'm going to have you, young man. Make this madam of wise old age want a healthy young stud like you."

Her fingers toyed with him and brought him to the fullness of himself.

"Nice! Real nice. I knew there was something nice about you, and now I'll find out."

After a few minutes she said, "More! More!"

He was thinking of her maid, picturing the beautiful woman he usually had in this position in this room.

She whispered again, "All older women enjoy the good hardness of a young man."

Blair felt her thrash beneath him, then seized him with her voice uttering French words, which he took to be signs of her pleasure. They were.

He lay relaxed beside her, then rose up to go.

"Where do you go, my good stud?"

"I've got to get back. You are happy, aren't you?"

She laughed, pulling him to her flabby breasts and body again. "This is not enough, Cherie. There are many other ways. I'm French, did I not tell you?"

He submitted to her advances, and be damned if she wasn't French!

They both lay back on the bed. She closed her eyes and whispered, "Love me, my Cherie."

She felt his mouth upon her breast. Her body became fully awake at the feel of Blair's hot tongue, stabbing and thrashing. She wanted to cry out but was gripped with a new feeling of ecstasy. She wanted him to stop, but didn't want the feeling to ever stop. She couldn't resist the wracking pleasure that he brought to every fiber of her body. His fast, smooth, undulating tongue was demanding response. She fought it, but was brought under its thrilling control.

"Oh! Oh! My Cherie!"

He didn't answer. With quick movement of her damp body she arched up and trembled violently as she placed her hands on the back of his head and held it there. She was seized with the ferocious desire to smother him. Her thighs squeezed him in a vice.

She quivered and screamed, "Stop, my Cherie. Oh, Cherie, for God's sake, stop. You're killing me, my Cherie. I can't stand it any longer. Please! Please! Sto..." Her body jerked as her navel trembled and she was torn apart by the tremendous sweet force. His hands lay on her belly and pressed down gently as she groaned and fainted. Only then did her thighs relax and release him. He breathed and gasped frantically trying to return to normal.

Before he had gotten dressed and ready to leave Madam LaCall had said, "Now I know why Emma stays here. I had wondered. And believe me, she's a smart nigger. But, tell me, Cherie, what part of France did you say you were from?"

***

At the dairy ranch, Clay was getting ready to return to town, having looked in on Kate. Leaving the others, he glanced back at the ranch house and saw the one lighted room.

His thought became black as he decided to try out his first plan. Other thoughts crowded this from his mind, letting Kate's accident remain foremost.

He knew Kate to be forthright in her thinking, yet he wondered if Kate had meant what she'd said, wishing she had been wise enough to plan the accident. "Why that black son of a bitch," thought Clay. "Oh, hell, if she really meant it, Diamond's got himself a good woman."

These things began to twiddle at him, and he fought to control himself. He had heard and had seen black and white together, but he wondered if it made them feel the same way it was making him feel. He would ask Kate about it, knowing she would tell him the truth.

Riding along, he became obsessed and angry for his little thought. And, to him, they were really little. Or was he small?

NINETEEN

When Kate was able to ride again, which was a couple of days later, she left early in the morning, but not before she'd seen Cliff alone and made arrangements to see him later in the week.

Pet decided to ride with her part of the way. They both said goodbye to Diamond and rode towards Pueblo.

Pet returned, laughing to herself at the things Kate had told her. Some of the thoughts even caused her to blush. She returned in time to help check the dairy products that were being shipped out. Pet took a large slice of cheese and some butter into the house with her.

Her father was still in bed. The hour was early, only about 7:30a.m. Since she didn't have too much work to do in the house, she went to work in the newly planted flowerbed. Her father, when he awoke, could see her from his room. She was humming a tune when Diamond came and looked at the flowers. She glanced up at his boldness and remarked, "All done in the barn?"

"Uh-huh. Think maybe I'll help you. I kinda like

flowers myself."

"All right, start right in."

He bent down to his knees and started right in help-ing. The two worked side by side, not knowing that their father was watching. In silence they worked, Pet still humming to herself and thinking about the Negro working worth her. He was polite to her, but most niggers were she reflected. She looked up once to see him looking rather hard at her. She said nothing. He was not even smiling, but when she looked up again he was grinning. This made her face redden and she felt as if he was violating her with his eyes.

She demanded furiously, "What are you looking at?"

"I was just thinking how pretty you are. A man like..."

He was going to say Clay, but she interrupted him. Glaring at him she said, "Why don't you niggers stay in your place!"

This hurt more coming from her, but he said, "I'm in my place here with you and..."

Before he could finish Pet jumped up. He looked at her and felt the sting of her naked hand flush across his face and mouth. Her hands were dirty and dirt was left clinging to his lips. Then she spat at him saying, "You nigger son of a bitch!"

He was hurt, dazed and halted but knew she just didn't understand. How could she when she didn't even know they shared a father?

He slowly came to his feet and walked to the fence, where he leaned looking out into the pasture, feeling rejected and misunderstood. Tears streamed down his face and he wasn't ashamed of them. He felt only pity for his half-sister. In his heart he just wanted to tell her everything.

Mr. Phillips, having witnessed the entire scene, felt his heart sink. The misery of a hundred years fell upon him in this single moment. He had to tell Pet, not only for her sake but for Diamond's, too. He knew his son was hurt in a way no stranger could hurt him.

He called Pet into his room. She was crying.

"My baby, what's wrong?"

"Dad, get that nigger away from here."

"Why?"

"Why? Because he said some things to me that were insulting to any decent white woman."

Her father knew how wrong she was, but wanted her to repeat the remarks.

"Well, what did he say?"

She dried her eyes and told him.

Mr. Phillips drew himself up in bed and said, "Here, baby, sit here."

She looked at her father, knowing he would do as she asked and baby her along.

"Pet," he began, the words coming from a choked voice that had a painful thing to explain, an enigma which might not be understood. "Pet, Cliff had every right to say you are pretty and that he had a right to be here and is in his place."

She jumped from her father's bed with indignation and disgust yelling, "Dad, how could you say that about a nigger?"

He was hurt by his daughter's words. By insulting Diamond she was insulting him as well.

"Pet, don't you think any son, black or white, has the right to be with his father and sister?"

Pet gasped and her jaw sagged as if someone had

THE ULTIMATE WESTERN NOVEL

hit her in the pit of the stomach. She wavered and, dizzily, staggered to the bed, sliding to her knees onto the floor sobbing her heart out and crying, "Dad, oh, no! Not a nigger son, Dad? Oh, Dad, how could you hurt me so? Oh, Dad."

Her father let her cry as he looked out the window at his son standing by the fence. He saw Pet was becoming hysterical and yelled, "Cliff! Yo, Cliff!"

Diamond heard his father call and ran into the room, seeing Pet in a state of insanity. He met his father's eyes and asked, "You told her, Pa?"

"Yeah. Her shock is genuine. But after she slapped you, I felt she had to know the truth before she hurt us all beyond repair."

Diamond kneeled down and picked up his half sister, laying her on the bed from which his father had just gotten up.

"Just lay her there, she'll be all right," said his father.

Diamond couldn't help but to kiss Pet's cheek. When his father saw it, he moaned as the tears streamed down his face. Instantly Diamond forgave his half sister and they knew it. That's what had touched him so much.

Mr. Phillips dressed and sat down beside his daughter, holding her hand. Diamond put his hand on his father's shoulder saying, "Pa, you did what you had to do. Don't blame yourself. We are your children by birth, and you were honest when we were conceived. We couldn't have asked for more."

The load seemed lightened by his son's consoling words. Mr. Phillips said, "Yes, there was nothing deceitful about either of you. My only regret is that I didn't tell her about you sooner."

"Maybe you still did the best thing."

"Maybe, son, and maybe not. God only knows. How glad I am that she knows now."

Pet finally got control of herself and just lay there looking at her father and half brother. They couldn't define the look in her eyes.

Mr. Phillips said, "Now the secret is open." He looked at both and continued, "Know this, Pet. I married Cliff's mother first, then I married your mother."

Whether she believed him or even heard him, he couldn't tell.

The was a moment without words, all having been said.

Suddenly she alighted from the bed and said, "I don't know when I'll be back, if ever."

"Pet!" cried Diamond reaching for her.

She shied away from him.

Their father calmly said, "Let her go, Cliff. I think she'll be all right."

All the way into town she cried and felt sorry for herself. But who could she turn to? Kate? No. She didn't want anyone to know. Clay? Maybe, just maybe. She knew she needed to talk to somebody.

In town she went directly to the jail office, hoping that Clay would be there but he wasn't. He was out, she learned from Old John. She sat in a chair and cried some more, asking him to "Please, go find him."

Old John found Clay at the station, where he'd gotten his expected package of things he wanted from his uncle in Austin, plus another wire that read:

> *Clay*
>
> *Am confirming first report. As stated, three land grants in Colorado area; Grant One, the largest, to*

Julius Harmsley Lee and heirs; Grant Two to Daniel Armstrong rescinded; Grant three to John Derrymore of Pueblo to points fifty miles or more in all directions. Am expecting to hear of your success soon.

    Sincerely,
    Uncle Mart

Clay was glad to receive the news from his uncle. It made a lot of things clear and now he could move on. He already knew Billy Ferrell was suspected of being a member of the gang, but what his uncle Mart didn't know was that Clay knew exactly who Billy was – and the gang. He was feeling jubilant when Old John came over to him and told him about Pet crying at the office. Half running, half walking, Clay went to Pet.

She had managed to dry her face, but still looked the worst from the crying.

He said excitedly, "What happened out at the ranch?"

She broke down again. Clay walked over and closed the door, taking her in his arms. She felt at ease, secure from the world of hard facts. He teased her by feeling through her skirt. She didn't respond, even when he nuzzled her breasts.

"Jesus, Pet, it can't be that bad!"

"That's what you think!"

"Well, tell me about it."

"How can I tell you my father is Cliff's father, too."

"Oh, so you found out about that."

"Found out!" she exclaimed, surprised at his knowing.

"I guess you had to sooner or later."

"Well. I didn't think you'd take a nigger for a

brother-in-law so calmly."

"Pet, can't you stop saying nigger now that you know Cliff is a blood relative?"

"He's no relative of mine. He's just my father's, who, I think, cheated me by holding out what I should have been told."

"Pet, don't you know he wanted to protect you until you were old enough to understand?"

"Well, I understand both my father and his nigger son."

"Pet!" he exclaimed, becoming angry at her outburst.

"Don't you Pet me, it's true! I've got a nigger for a brother, and I should be proud like Kate? Let me tell you, Mr. Clay Clinton, never, never, never will a nigger make me proud – brother or father or a nigger mother!"

"You shouldn't say things you don't really mean, Pet."

"Don't worry, Clay, I mean them. How would you like a nigger to tell your sister she's pretty?"

"That's quite enough out of you, young lady!"

"Enough of what? I think you're a sissy, catering to that Negro. Hell, you got nigger blood in you too?"

After she had finished her remark Clay answered, to the point of showing he was not to be outdone. Calmly he took her by the waist and, taking a chair, turned her over his knee and said, "You should have had this a long time ago."

He applied his hand to the softness of her round buttocks and, in measured rapid strokes, spanked her. She yelled and cursed him but it made no difference. He didn't stop until he felt the point was driven home.

She fell to the floor. He only looked at her without

going near her. When she stopped crying, she rubbed her sore backside and could hardly stand to touch herself.

Clay said, "Maybe that will teach you a lesson."

She was angry, but feared another lesson so she stuck her tongue out at him.

"Now, get up off the floor!" Clay demanded.

She obeyed instantly like an obedient child. Clay didn't apologize to her or even appear to be sorry. She, on the other hand, was proud of him and knew just how far she could go.

Clay realized he had to talk to her. He gave her a moment, and then began by saying, "Listen to me and don't interrupt." He was stern, almost like a father, but he felt what he had to say was of great importance. "Pet, I think I know how you feel. And, I think we both pride ourselves on being fair without hate toward a Negro or anyone else. That's because we were on the other side looking in. But now that same position is here, and inevitably connected to us and we've found out how prejudiced we really are. I explained to Diamond that a close connection with him was new to me, too and that it was only natural to make mistakes. And so are you, Pet. Diamond realized this and is big enough to forgive us. Then, on the other hand, you and I must realize that Cliff, too, has a hatred for whites that he fights to keep back. He just does a better job than we do. He had to accept a white father, knowing he had no choice to pick a color. I'm telling you this, Pet, because right now you can cause a hell of a lot of damage. You could cause your brother to hate you and your father and you, in turn, could come to hate me. I know that I am that close to you. Frankly, Pet, I realize that I'm not perfect. I hate to admit it, but I conceded to accept your brother as a friend and I think I've become a better man by doing so. You would be a better woman if you did the same. Our trouble is that we worry about what others will think, but you didn't hesitate to offer a place in your father's hotel for Cliff that night he came into town and into our lives. Do you really care what others think or what I think? That's what counts."

Pet had listened to the long speech and thought of what Clay said to her. She saw herself talking to Diamond and saw her father's face upon them. She loved her father, and could see his love for his son.

As she thought, without raising her head, she asked, "Come to think of the matter and really look at it, you can see how much Diamond looks like Dad. Can you see it, Clay?"

"I have. And, you and Diamond have got similar features as well. 'Course, I'm more interested in your features."

She smiled for the first time and Clay embraced her. She clung to him tightly saying, "Clay, help guide me through this. I trust you to lead me right."

"We'll go through this together. Just remember, your brother has feelings the same as we do."

"My brother!" she exclaimed.

"Can you accept him, Pet?"

After a long pause she said, "How do you mean, Clay?"

"I mean, can you find a place in your heart and in your family where he belongs."

"Well," she said, "let's put it this way. I've done some things that weren't right, so Cliff will just have to forgive me. Depending on that, I'll know if he's my brother or just another man."

Clay was satisfied with her conclusion. He kissed her and she returned it, placing one of his hands where she thought it ought to be. She said, "If you keep neglecting me, I'll never forgive you."

He smiled and drew her closer.

TWENTY

While everyone else went back about their business in Pueblo, Blair Tyson and his boys went about theirs. They had met in Blair's office where he had given them their assignments. Each man knew the job he was expected to do. The first of July was only three days away, which would still give the men plenty of time to be in their positions for the coming robbery.

The men had left Blair's office in pairs, leaving only Texas Red Morgan and Blair still in the office. All had agreed to still give Hank his share even though he was laid up with the two busted shoulders from Diamond's guns. As usual, when they went out on a job, they had their alibis all worked out. They would be out working on Bryant's spread. Who would question the word of the banker?

Blair and Texas Red left the office and went over to the bank. They only stayed a few minutes. This was in preparation of establishing an alibi for Blair and Texas Red. Naturally, the banker had the setup down pat.

Leaving the bank they went to the Payday. Texas Red checked his guns and laughed, knowing Blair still wore his hidden one.

This was the first time Blair had seen Kate since her bout with the rattler. He spoke to her and she returned his greeting. She said nothing to Texas Red, nor did he to her.

Blair, after ordering a bottle and taking a few drinks with Texas Red, moved from the bar to Kate's table saying, "How's the thigh?"

"Fine now, Blair." Kate noticed his eyes.

"Come on in the office, Kate. I want to talk to you."

"What about?"

"Will you come on?"

She led the way behind the bar to her little office.

The Payday wasn't too crowded this morning, only a few miners were there getting ready to go to Leadville on the next train. The girls all sat around, lazily waiting for business while chatting and filing their fingernails.

LeeLee had crossed her flashy legs, resting her ankle on her knee to tie her boot. Texas Red was looking at the movement and kept his eyes glued up her dress. She let her foot slide to the floor and looked around to see Texas Red's flushed face. She knew he'd seen under her dress, but dismissed it with a frown. She walked from the table straight over to him and said, "Did you like what you saw? Or didn't you see enough?"

"What I saw was what I wanted to see!"

"All right. Then pay for it and it's yours for a little while."

"I don't pay!"

"You sure as hell don't get it for free."

Texas Red laughed. She walked back to her table leaving him to think. Yet, she somehow knew he was already satisfied.

Blair sat on the edge of Kate's desk. He tried to be calm, but was flustered. "How did you enjoy your stay at the ranch?"

"Quite well."

"The reason I ask is, I'm going to Leadville for a few days and I thought you might like to go along with me."

This statement was not like him. Kate figured he had a reason for asking.

"No, I'll stay here. There's nothing in Leadville for me."

"Yeah, I guess so, it's out there at the Phillips' ranch, eh?"

"Just what in the hell do you mean by that, Blair?"

"Just what I said. You must have been crazy under that nigger out there."

"If you mean Diamond..."

"If I mean Diamond? Who in the hell else could I mean?"

"Listen Blair, I know what you're thinking, and it's not true."

"Tell me something, Kate..."

Filled with fury Kate slammed back, "Yeah, let me tell you something, Blair. You don't own me just because you had me in bed a few times."

"Listen, Kate, I just don't like the idea of a black nigger smelling around a white woman."

Kate only laughed. "You should talk, when everybody in town knows how you sneak in to Madam LaCall's shop to get her black maid."

"That cow," he said.

"Yeah, I'm a bitch to you, but you can bet on one thing, if I could get under him I would. He'd be a welcome relief from your slobbering."

He became furious and with red rage, slapped her

hard across the face, shook her and yelled, "When we finish this job, we'll take care of that nigger and you, too!"

Kate screamed back at him, "Since I'm already accused of giving it to Diamond, I might as well go right on ahead and do it. And damn you or anyone else who doesn't like it."

Blair stormed out of the office. Texas Red got his guns and they both rushed out of the Payday on their way according to plans.

LeeLee rushed into Kate's office when Blair left. She saw Kate was crying and tried to talk to her.

"Kate!"

Kate looked up and she knew some of the conversation between Blair and herself must have been heard outside the office. LeeLee brought her a cold towel. Kate wiped her face and said, "LeeLee, you know many a man has gone to hell for that funny little fluff between a woman's legs, especially when they think they own it."

"I know, Kate. But if you ask me, Blair's already on his way to hell, with Texas Red right along with him."

Kate looked up, then said, "LeeLee, don't mention this to anyone."

"I won't, Kate, but these things have a way of getting around."

"I know. I just hope Blair stays away from Diamond."

"He won't. Not after the way you told him how you'd rather have Diamond than him."

"It's the truth, LeeLee, and you know it."

"I think so."

"I'm to meet him soon. He'll know how I feel then.

I'll see to that for sure."

"Good girl, Kate. And when you do, wait till he gets a big hump in his back, then say to yourself, 'That's one for you LeeLee!' I may even feel it."

Kate laughed in appreciation of LeeLee's friendship. LeeLee knew what she was talking about, and Kate admired her common sense. At least in their business, frankness was a virtue.

**

When Pet left Clay, she started in to see Kate but then changed her mind after seeing Blair and Texas Red going into the Payday. Instead, she stopped and bought a few things. Among them was a pair of silver spurs and a pongee shirt. She also checked the station for mail. While there she saw Madam LaCall's maid who'd just gotten off the morning train from Denver.

Pet, laden with packages said, "Hi, Emma!"

"Hello, Miss Pet."

Pet learned that Emma had been to Denver for the madam.

Pet came back to the ranch during the middle of the afternoon. It was hot with no sign of relief. With everything under consideration after she had talked with Clay, she felt better. She made no pretense at what she had to do, she felt she had to make things right. Seeing no one around the house or barn, she urged her little painted mare across the fording place in the stream that served the springhouse.

Back at the house, she dismounted from her horse, laid her packages on the porch and then returned to her mount to remove the saddle and bridle. The little trained mare nudged her along to the pasture gate.

"All right! All right! Take your time, girl," Pet said

to the horse. She laughed at the horse pushing her. Pet opened the gate and the mare kicked up its feet and jumped around, running free with the other horses. Pet watched for a moment and thoughts of freedom flooded her mind.

Picking up her packages, she went into the house. She didn't see her farther around. She washed and changed into a different skirt and blouse. After looking at herself, she swished out to find her family calling, "Dad!" There was no answer.

She heard gunfire and looked towards the sound. Seeing nothing, she went back to the parlor where she sat and looked out the window at her flowerbed. She smiled to herself, thinking everything would work out.

Then she heard her father's footsteps. He was evidently talking to Diamond.

She called, "Dad, is Cliff out there?"

"Yep. What do you want?"

"Ask him to come in here, please. And you come too! I didn't see anyone around when I came home."

"What did you want, Pet?"

Pet glanced at the packages on the desk and, wringing her hands said, "I'm no good at this sort of thing, but, Dad, I'm real sorry about this morning."

"I knew that you would be after you'd had some time to think it over."

"I know it doesn't make up for my behavior, but I've brought you both a peace offering." She got up and handed each of them a package, the shirt to her father and the spurs to her brother.

When the two men unwrapped their gifts and looked at each other in amazement they said, almost simultaneously, "Thank you, Pet!"

Mr. Phillips was quick to realize this was an important gesture between his children and remarked, jokingly, "So, neither of you want the old man around I suppose. I'll get on out of here and let you be."

All three smiled.

Her brother sat on the corner of the desk, mostly leaning against it. He laid his new spurs on the desk and spoke first. "I'll be real proud to wear these."

"I'm glad you like them, Cliff. I want to tell you how sorry I am for..."

"I understand, Pet."

"No, Cliff, I don't think you do. You see, I had a good talk with Clay," she said, rubbing her seat, "and he spanked some sense into me."

"You mean he actually spanked you?"

"Yep, he turned me right over his knee and spanked my tail good."

"Clay's quite a man," laughed her brother.

She blushed, agreeing with him, and said, "I'm here to tell you!"

She thrust her hands into the pockets of her skirt and continued. "Cliff, I was a nasty little bitch this morning, but if you'll forgive me, I'll honestly try to be as much of a sister to you as you are a brother to me."

Diamond was touched and felt compassion for her plea.

"I guess it's hard on you, Pet, the shock of it all, but I'm rather pleased to have you for a sister."

"Cliff, please understand, all of those names, black and nigger, I didn't mean any of them. I don't even know what they mean. I've heard the other nig... I mean Negroes call each other those names and I never thought about their meaning much. From now on, I'll try not to use those words."

"Pet, you're something like me, in a way. I like your frankness. I don't think I'd want a sister who was a prissy little thing. I like your spirit, so let's forget all of that this morning. I realize it may be hard for you as well as for me, but I don't think it can throw either of us."

She agreed to his statement and found it to be as Clay had said. Turns out it was hard for Diamond, too.

Pet couldn't be all-forgiving, Diamond knew, but she was helping both of them become more appreciative of the other. His sister had her mind made up to accept him as a brother and, when she thought of everything as a whole, she felt proud of the fact. It was with this attitude in mind that she spoke, by way of letting him know her guard was completely down.

"When a brother and sister find each other, shouldn't they show it?"

"Maybe so," said Cliff, "but how?"

"Well, I always thought a family kiss was in order."

He came to her and held her arms in his strong hand and kissed her on the cheek.

"You call that a kiss?" she laughed and raised her small lips up to him. He tenderly kissed them.

She added words to tease him, "So, you see, it's really not right, but I know you didn't kiss Kate like that!"

"Pet!"

"Don't 'Pet' me. You know you kissed her and so do I."

He couldn't explain it. There was no use.

"Oh well, I guess she told you. So now you know."

"We women talk to each other, remember. Anyway, you need a woman and Kate needs a man, and I believe she's got one, eh, Cliff?"

"Pet, after all I..."

"Yeah, I know. After all."

She laughed at his being on the defensive and in an uncomfortable position. She didn't know Cliff had a date with Kate later that same night. He was squirming to no end. But they had a good understanding, a new friendship. This would be their family, the three of them together with their father leading the way.

***

Later that night Diamond was to meet Kate down by the river in a little wooded section. When he arrived, Kate was already waiting for him. He told her how he and Pet had come to an understanding.

Kate's closeness aroused him. He reached for her and she tumbled into his arms. Their lips met as his hand squeezed one of her breasts tenderly. She became restless and moved to the touch of his fingers. Diamond dropped his hand from her breast, but she grabbed his arms and said, "Cliff, don't let me go on feeling like this."

He looked at her thoughtfully and said, "I want you, Kate. Do you really want me? Do you realize what it will mean?"

"Don't you see I can't fight against you anymore, Cliff? Can't you see I want to be fondled and satisfied by you – just you?"

They were seated upon a large log. She lay in his arms. He kissed her hard and felt her shudder and then relax. He slipped her dress above her thighs and, in the dim light of the moon, his eyes enjoyed the feast of looking at her half-covered body. His hands pressed gently as he moved them over her legs. Kate twitched in anticipation of more. He enjoyed the entertaining sigh of the clouded pinkness of her thighs showing through the tiny mesh panties. She rose up and slipped the flimsy covering to her knees.

"Damn it, Cliff, I can't stand it any longer. I want you!"

He grabbed her and laid her down upon the grass. She raised her dress high above her waist saying, "Here, my darling, take what is yours."

He kissed her hard, sinking his teeth into her flesh as he rolled on top of her. She felt him slip within her as the full power of his body thrust tight upon hers.

"Oh, God!" she breathed. "Cliff, do it. I want all of you, every black inch of you, my darling!"

She arched her body to meet his movements. With damp bodies, they moved like savages: one black, one white, blending into a pile of confusion. Passion swept through them.

He whispered, "Kate from now on you're my woman and I'm your man."

"Yes, oh, yes, my darling... Oh, faster, Cliff. Faster..."

In a fit of frenzy they called each other sweet, endearing names. No one else was around, and their satisfaction was to please each other. Cliff's knees began to buckle form the force of relief and he knew that Kate had also reached her own climax as she clawed and bit to the edge of a calm, sweet – oh, so sweet – and peaceful feeling.

He released her and she kissed him. They lay there together, both knowing and realizing what it meant to be with someone you really love.

They saw the moon peaking through the trees and heard fish splashing in the nearby river. Everything in the world was peaceful, Cliff and Kate the most peaceful of all.

TWENTY-ONE

The general atmosphere in Pueblo was good. Mr. Phillips had told his son how things were working out. At least the people of Pueblo were not against him.

This left a factor of trouble in only one place, Blair his men and the banker.

However, at the ranch there was complete harmony. The few men employed at Phillips' ranch took a liking to Diamond, with the exception of Sandy who had quit when the Negro first came to work there. On different occasions the dairy workmen had heard of Diamond's troubles with the Blair outfit. When they asked Mr. Phillips about it, he explained it to them. He said that most of the workmen here were of some extraction and, if it came to a fight, they were a hell-bent crew. Diamond was always present at these discussions and it never made a big difference to the operation of the ranch.

Clay, meanwhile, stayed in town, with his eyes alert for trouble. He had conceded to himself that when the trouble did break he could forget about his threat to ram them bloomers down Blair's throat as well as Blair's men as he had promised, but still the idea wasn't completely forgotten. He knew just about where the pieces of the puzzle went and how they fit together.

In talking to folks, he'd learned that Blair mentioned something about the job to be done and that Texas Red Morgan had gone to Leadville. The most important thing he knew was that the land grant information from his uncle was Blair's backbone. Whatever else he had in mind, he hardly believed that Blair was the true owner, but knew, as a smart lawyer, he had ways of fighting and fixing those things.

His mind turned to the banker. He was tied in some way, and it was his belief that the banker was in on everything Blair did. The bank would be a perfect place to put stolen money into circulation.

All those things had to be proven. Even the money Kate had banked and written a check for had turned out to be stolen.

Mr. Phillips, when he'd cashed the two thousand dollar check and brought the money in gold to Clay, had been surprised when Clay told him the gold double eagles were part of a shipment stolen a few months ago in Arizona.

Mr. Phillips asked, "But who?"

Clay couldn't tell him, simply because he didn't know. However, in his mind, he was sure it was tied to Blair and his men.

Marshal Clay Clinton had walked around town putting everything into place. Visiting the Payday and the Dipper saloons as well as the other places, he made a deliberate search of the town from end to end and side to side but couldn't find any of Blair's men anywhere. This puzzled him. It was the first time he'd seen or known of the whole crew being out of town at one time.

He thought about the Bryant ranch. To keep suspicion down, he told Old John to ride out there with a message.

Old John returned and said there was no one on the place.

"No one, John? Are you sure?"

"Not nary a soul, and I even rode around the ranch for a spell."

This was strange for any ranch. Hardly ever would a place be completely abandoned. Still, it added fire to Clay's thoughts.

Clay still wasn't satisfied and rode out to check for himself. He had ridden in the back way and saw a lone shack with light swirls of smoke coming from the chimney.

He stepped down from his horse and proceeded through the cover of woods to within a few feet of the building. He listened and heard nothing so he advanced to peep through a crack in the wall. He could make out one man lying in a bunk, the upper parts of his body covered with bandages. "That has to be Hank," he thought. The three men sitting at the broken table he'd never seen before.

He heard one of the men say, "That nigger who shot your brother must be real slick, Ripper."

"We'll see how slick he is when we meet him," Ripper replied.

Since there was no light in the shack and the trees made dark shadows, Clay couldn't see very clearly but he had heard enough. He carefully slipped back away from the shack. A horse he couldn't see whinnied, then another. Clay moved with swift speed into the cover of the woods. The whinnying from the horses brought the three men from the shack.

Clay had just mounted Baldy and was headed out when he heard a yell, "There goes somebody!"

A hail of gunfire followed, carrying death through the leaves on the trees, a few landing with a dull thud into the trunk of the tree where Clay had been just seconds before. Baldy took the unbroken trail as if he knew every inch of ground. Clay looked back, but could see no one following. He was thankful for the cover of the pinion woods and spruce.

***

Back from his trip and now in his office, Clay was satisfied. What he had heard at the shack on the Bryant spread didn't cause him worry, unless Diamond came into town. He laughed to himself thinking about how things fell into place when not rushed. Again, he went out into the streets of Pueblo to look around and be on hand for whatever might come about.

Later in the evening, when the work at the dairy ranch was brought underway, Mr. Phillips, his son and his daughter came into town. Mr. Phillips and Pet went to the hotel. Diamond lingered there for a few minutes, then went over to the Payday Casino.

As a law-abiding citizen, Diamond checked his guns with Sam, the bartender, before ordering a glass of his father's product – milk – into which he poured two shots of strong branch. Sam laughed.

The patrons of the Payday paid Diamond no mind. They were getting used to seeing him there. They considered him none of their affair, except LeeLee, who bounced up on the bar and flashed Diamond one of her prettiest smiles.

She looked at Diamond's drink and said, laughing,

"Don't be so tight with your moo juice."

"Give the lady exactly what I'm having, Sam."

Sam, faithful to his job, blended the strong branch with milk and sat it in front of LeeLee who frowned, thinking it was plain milk.

"Oh, didn't you know I'm a big girl now. Or is it when you buy a drink it's always back to mother's breasts?"

Diamond laughed.

LeeLee added, "Hell, maybe a change to milk will do something for me."

"It will. Go ahead and try it," Diamond said.

LeeLee took the first drink totally unprepared. She yelled, laughing, "My God, what a cow!"

"I thought you might like it."

LeeLee looked at him and said, "I know you're not buying, but the boss lady isn't feeling too good."

One of the girls was playing a honky tonk blues on the piano while LeeLee and Diamond chatted. LeeLee thanked him for the drink and flirted away to other likely customers when three tall, wide-shouldered men came into the saloon.

They paused at the door, observing the Negro still sipping his milk. The shortest of the group nudged his nearest partner. They nodded their heads in agreement.

Kate had just come downstairs and was making her way to the three men. She passed Diamond and said, "Stick around, I want to talk to you."

"Will do, Kate."

She greeted the new men saying gaily, "Come on in, boys. You must be new around here. You've got to check that hardware your carrying."

"All right, sister, we'll come in. But the hardware

stays put."

"No, no boys. Not in here. It's town law by order of the marshal."

"Yeah, we heard about fancy vest and his pretty pink bloomers."

Diamond remained seated at the bar and gave Sam a look. He could see the men in the mirror behind the bar.

Kate said again, "Come on, fellow, have a good time but check the guns."

"Like we said, sister, we'll treat you real nice but the iron stays."

Two of the men advanced to the bar while the third one stood by the door with his eyes glued on Sam, the barkeeper. One of the men at the bar placed his money down and, looking in the mirror straight at Diamond, said, "Didn't know you white folks rubbed elbows with niggers. Barkeep, put a bottle on the bar."

Kate knew they were on the prowl, so did Diamond.

Sam said, "No bottle till them guns is checked."

The man standing by the door replied, "set that bottle on the bar, mister, and leave that scatter gun there where it is. Understand?"

Kate nodded her head to Sam, thinking this might ease the matter. The bottle was placed on the bar. The two men moved closer to Diamond and poured their drinks.

"Here, nigger, have a drink!"

The man who ordered didn't wait for an answer but poured some whiskey in Diamond's milk. The other man, with his side to the bar, remarked, "You look like a man, so drink a man's drink. Milk is for tit babies."

The few card players stopped playing cards and,

with a feeling of impending trouble in the air, everyone else in the Payday became quiet. Cautiously, the man playing the piano stopped and was peering out over top of it.

Diamond, pushing the glass away, said, "I've had enough to drink."

"Now that's Diamond unsociable," muttered the shortest one.

The men were agitating, but as of yet, Diamond remained calm. The man who had poured the drink moved closer and hit Diamond's foot. Everybody saw what was going on, but no one was going to go up against three pairs of guns.

"Look out, boy, you stepped on my foot!"

Diamond smiled for the first time and said, "Excuse me."

"Excuse you, my ass! Watch where you're going."

The other two men called out, "Hey, Ripper, I don't think he's sorry."

"You shouldn't have stepped on my foot, nigger. I've got corns."

"In that case you should teach them how to dodge."

The two men needling him resented his remark, but laughed.

The onlookers gasped in awe at the coolness of the sharp remark Diamond slammed back at the troublemakers.

Kate saw a man ease towards the door and heard the guard say, "Sit down, mister, unless you're tired of growing old."

Diamond knew that this was a squeeze play and no one was to be let out. He wondered where Clay was. He was trapped, overpowered and almost helpless.

The guard at the door yelled, "Hey, Ripper, since this is a private party, let's have the black boy do a little dance for us to liven things up!"

Ripper threw down his gun. Diamond turned from the bar facing him. The man fired shots near his feet and laughed saying, "Dance, nigger!"

Diamond could feel the floor vibrate where the bullets opened splintered holes near his feet but he didn't move a muscle, saying grimly, "I don't dance."

"Well, you better start singing, boy!" said Ripper.

Kate couldn't stand it any longer and stepped in to plead with the men. She stood a little to the side of Diamond, who said, "Don't beg them, Kate."

"But Diamond, they..."

The short man cut right in, "Will you listen to that? A black bastard pulling a white woman's skirt. How 'bout that, Ripper?"

"We'll see!"

He reached for Kate's arm and grabbed her, patted her on the ass and hips and said, "Now, I'll bet this is a pretty good lay, huh, girlie."

Diamond's mind was fast at work. He figured either Clay had heard the shots or someone else hearing them had gone to find Clay and tell him. In either event, it would bring him running. But he couldn't let him walk into a squeeze. He did a bold thing, as his calmness dictated.

"Take your stinking hands off her."

Kate almost went limp. This was an open declaration of how he felt.

LeeLee almost jerked her head up in admiration, knowing the men had done the wrong thing in touching Kate.

Diamond repeated his demand. "I said, take your stinking hands off her."

"And if I don't, nigger?"

"Then I'll take them off for you."

"A nigger who wants a white woman, Ripper!"

"Yeah, they all do, but this is the first one I've ever seen admit it."

As if by prearrangement, Kate looked at Cliff. He motioned with his eyes. She looked at him in a special way, to show that she understood his instructions.

Kate heard the three men laughing at the last remark and knew they had, for a split second, relaxed. She stomped her heel hard on the foot of the man holding her. He yelled and she broke away from his hold. She said a silent prayer for Diamond, for she knew all hell would break loose, led by the devil himself.

This is what Diamond had asked Kate for with his eyes. The second Kate moved from the man, Diamond moved in, catching the man in front of him by the arm. A bullet whizzed past his shoulders. With the strength of a tiger, Diamond twisted the man around with his right hand, moving like lightning. He lifted the man's left hand gun from its holster.

The guard by the door yelled, "Drop, Ripper."

The other man, who was moving backwards towards the door, snapped off two more shots, which Diamond avoided by pushing his captive into the direct line of fire. The heavy slugs slammed into the man and tore through his body. Out of the corner of his eye, Diamond saw the guard bringing his gun up. He fell to the floor and rolled towards where he'd been. Within that same second, the guard by the door took three slugs, all in the chest, from Diamond's now flaming guns.

The third man was going through the door. Diamond's last two bullets slammed into the swinging door. The retreating gunman had scored a hit with his parting shot, grazing the agile Negro along his side.

Outside the door Clay came running up and called, "Hold it!"

The running gunman turned, gun in hand. Clay's guns spoke with thundering smoke and flame. The man spun around and crashed back through the swinging doors of the Payday Casino. Clay stood over the dead man. He saw the other two fallen comrades.

Diamond was on his feet. Kate was feverishly tearing away his shirt to see where he was hit. They said nothing as Kate led Diamond to her little office.

Bedlam broke out. Because the action had been so swift, no one could believe what they'd just seen. They all crowded around the marshal, looking at the three dead men and explaining how everything had happened.

One old timer said, "Marshal, I'd rather that black boy side with me than any ten men."

There was no doubt in Clay's mind that Diamond had been at a great disadvantage. He asked Sam something.

Sam explained, "Hell, Marshal, Diamond's guns are still hanging there. Look!"

"They sure are," replied another onlooker.

Since Clay had been out to the Bryant ranch, he knew these three men were out to get Diamond, especially Hank's brother, the one called Ripper.

LeeLee came over to Clay and, as everyone else had done, explained the whole situation with her last remark ringing, "They made one mistake."

"What was that?"

"They touched Kate," she sighed.

Clay flushed at the suggestion. That gnawing feeling returned and he knew his control would have to overcome that one resentment.

Kate had bandaged Cliff's superficial wound. He was all right except for the stinging.

Kate stood looking at the giant of a man and was compelled to ask, "Cliff, why did you try to protect me? You know I'm a whore."

"Maybe because I feel the woman is better than the things she's done."

"Cliff, are you telling me that you care that much?"

"After that night by the river, yes, I guess I am."

She didn't need to hear any more. She was shameless in his arms and relished the secure strength of his returned kisses.

"To think I hated you for what I needed most."

She lingered in her sanctuary, proud that her own was indeed a man. Black? That was not to be questioned. And, without a doubt, all man.

The marshal came into her office, knocking first. He was stunned. When he closed the door, Diamond still held Kate, her black hair and white face lying on his brown chest. Clay felt let down. He knew what he saw was honest, but he could not forgive either Kate or Cliff. He wanted to walk right back out, or just sink through the floor. This was what he was afraid to face. Everything he'd ever heard about a black man projected, to protect the white woman from the arms of a nigger, his mixed emotions evident, yet sure.

Diamond saw his resentment and turmoil. He released Kate.

She, too, saw Clay's disgust and hatred come to the surface. What could she say to explain this to him? Then she thought and said, "Clay, it needs no explanation. What you see is how two people feel about each other."

Clay couldn't talk. Diamond said, "I guess you know what happened out front."

"Yeah, and I'm not blaming you," Clay said in a placid manner. He tried to remain calm in the face of these two people, these two friends. He questioned, "How long has this been going on, Kate?"

"I don't think that matters, do you? It's quite plain to see you don't like it."

"No, I guess I don't."

"I don't think there's anything anyone can do about it, Clay," she said.

Diamond knew then what had to take place. He handed Kate the gun he'd taken from Ripper and said, "Here's souvenir. Now leave us alone, Kate. And tell Sam not to let anybody interfere, no matter what."

He kissed her. She looked from one man to the other before going out. What she saw there were no words to describe.

TWENTY-TWO

No one knew what was said in the office between the two men, but from talk of the last gunfight Diamond had in the Payday, it was being said that the marshal seemed displeased.

Clark Bryant took advantage of the latest killings to push his citizen's committee since Blair wasn't in town. The meeting was to be held in the town station, which would hold at least fifty men.

On the night of the meeting, the men of the town all came. A few even brought their women to hear what the banker had to say. Moreover, the marshal was present. This was the aftermath of Diamond defending himself, but the banker was using it in two ways, to get rid of the marshal and the Negro and to arouse the citizens of Pueblo to his way of thinking.

Whether or not Diamond was aware of this meeting no one knew. Mr. Phillips didn't attend. Pet was in town, and so was Diamond. Mr. Graystone was present and other shop owners and businessmen were there. Even Madam LaCall came.

Since there were no trains at this time of night, it afforded Mr. Bryant an excellent chance to persuade the people without interruption. He waited until the little station was full and the open windows were filled with heads.

Standing on a box, the banker cleared his throat and began by declaring, "Now we have had three more killings at the hand of this black. I ask you again, without a lot of tripe, what are we going to do? We know the marshal won't lock this man up, nor will he run him out of town!"

All eyes turned towards Clay. Clay, standing in the back of the station, saw the eyes move to him and then slowly back to the speaker.

The banker continued, "I beg of us, as white citizens, to do something about this before we are all at the mercy of this black man's gun."

Someone in the back of the crowd stood up to be seen and said, "From what I gather, Bryant, those riders deserved killing."

"I know for a fact, had it been me, I'd have done the same thing," said another.

The sly old banker saw his plans falling through and directed his tongue in a different direction. "All right. Maybe they did deserve killing, but did this nigger have to protect Kate, a white woman?"

The men began to stir. This was arousing their interest.

Clay listened and observed while the banker, seeing his words take effect, continued, "I'm sure none of us would want to see our women spoken for by a man like this. Just think, he must have had a good reason for sticking his neck out. Could it be he's thinking in terms of having a white woman? Not in this town, he won't!"

A few men cheered. Mr. Graystone stood up and said, "Bryant, I don't think you know what you're talking about."

"Graystone, you're not welcome at this meeting. You condone Phillips and the marshal."

Mr. Graystone started to protest but was shouted down by jeering. "Sit down, Graystone, we want to hear more," a voice yelled.

The banker continued to rave and stir the men up, yet all he said still didn't really seem to be believed.

Clay saw Kate standing by the door. The banker had been so talkative he didn't see her appear. Clay nodded and said a quiet hello. She knew he was still miffed at seeing her kiss Diamond, and his very reason for being here was, in part, due to that feeling. She had just learned of the meeting from Sam, after Diamond had been in and left the bar headed back out to the ranch.

Kate listened until she heard the banker say, "And I say, let's show the marshal and this nigger our women are pure and we intend to keep them that way."

When Kate heard this she shouted, "I'll just bet you do!"

Every man turned in his seat to see Kate in a short white dress. She walked up to where the banker was. Putting her hands on her hips she said, "Get down on the floor where it becomes you, Bryant. I want to say something."

"Hurray for Kate!" chanted the crowd.

Kate stepped up on the box, looked at the crowd before her and said in a loud enough voice for all to hear, "I didn't know men could be so foolish as to listen to a thing like that." She pointed to Bryant. "This man is feeding you all a lot of junk. He talks bout preserving the virtues of a white woman and other such trash, all to get rid of two real men, one white and one a Negro. Why is he doing this? Maybe I should tell you, for I'd hate like hell to see some of your faces at the end of the marshal's or Diamond's gun.

"Better to get to the meat of your story, Kate, I wanna go home," somebody cried.

"Yeah, we all do," echoed another voice.

Again Kate started, "I think you all know my business, but I'm here for a different reason tonight. I'm here to remind you of who you all really are. To start with, Diamond is no less than any of you; he's a man, too. He didn't choose the color of his skin or his parents. I know. I thought differently about him myself when he first came to town, but after seeing the man and what he stands for, I dare say any one of you doesn't have the guts to do what he did. Besides that, I've done a hell of a lot of thinking, and it's my own belief and conclusion that white men say words to hear themselves talking. Now, listen, whether you like it or not, you white men have ruined everything you've touched. Look at the islands. Even in this country. You brought sickness and turmoil to the poor Indians when you took their land and gave them nothing but misery in return. You took their women for your own and, being tired of them, sent them back to their tribes in disgrace. You had Negro women for mistresses, which is a fashionable sport. The white man will let his wife and daughter employ the youthful Negro boy from ten to twelve years of age to be his wife's comfort and plaything. God only knows what these women have taught them, and so do I.

Above all, your grandparents and mine had become master of the black man and back then it was the black nannies who breast-fed your grandparent's children. Maybe some of you here were given life into frail, sickly bodies by suckling the breasts of robust, strong, healthy black women. And for this, your thanks is to exploit a black man because of his color.

So who are you to judge, when over half of you here are just two jumps ahead of the law yourself or else you wouldn't be here in this godforsaken hellhole?

I've been accused of being a black man's woman. If I am, that's my business. How many of you have come to my place sniffing around and getting my girls? Yes, with and without wives. I can name names if you'd like and tell you what you did and how much you paid for it. At least this black man you're all so quick to condemn hasn't been around my place looking to buy affection. He's honest enough to have a woman in the open, and if I'm that woman, it's my own damned business.

So how in the hell can you listen to Mr. Bryant and say you're protecting a woman's virtue? She'll protect her own. Some of you are even ruining your own women and you certainly know how. At least you come to my place to get what you can't or don't get at home. Come to Payday if you want to, but as far as I'm concerned every single one of you listening to this bastard makes me ashamed to be a white woman. If you don't believe me, ask your womenfolk, they'll tell you.

So Bryant, you can go to hell. The proverbial mistletoe is tied to my waist right around my backside. And, just to be neighborly, I warn you to be sure Diamond doesn't hear of this meeting or of your affront to me. He'll send you to hell faster than you can beg to differ."

Not only were there red faces but hurt pride and lots of condemned eyes as Kate walked from the box, her hips fully showing that she, indeed, was a woman.

The few women who were there stood up and cheered. One said, "It was a bit strong, like lye, Kate, but it's sure the truth. Come on Rufus!"

Bryant again took a position on the box and yelled, "Men! Men!"

"Get the hell down from that box before you break your neck, Bryant," called a voice.

"You can kiss my ass, too, you no-natured bastard," said another.

They all laughed at the man. He sat down, rejected and defeated. He knew it, but in his twisted mind, the blame went back to the black man and all who were connected to him.

When everyone had gone, the banker said aloud, "I'll kill him myself; he made a fool of me – him and his woman."

Clay hadn't left yet and he overheard Bryant's threat. "If you try, you can be sure you're on your way to tell the devil hello, Bryant. And it took a woman to send you there!"

All the hate the banker had for Diamond and Clay echoed in his threat. "You wait until Blair gets back. We'll string both of you sons of bitches up on a tree limb."

Clay laughed, but being duly informed of the gang's intentions replied, "I'll welcome the chance. Meantime, Bryant, try to have another meeting and see if the folks don't laugh you right out of town."

***

The Payday was doing a brisk business when Clay

arrived. He sorted Kate out of the crowd and said, "Do you believe what you said tonight?"

"Sure I do, Clay."

"I think you got a lot of men to see the right way, Kate, but I still can't figure you and Cliff."

"If you could forget Diamond is a black man, you'd figure it out. He needs a woman and I need a damn good man! I've found him. But actually, Clay, he's a little afraid of me."

"I don't blame him. And, Kate, I'm sorry for the way I acted the other night, but…"

"Hold it!" said Kate. "Don't explain to me, Clay. Tell Cliff, he's the one your hurt."

"Hell, Kate, I told him I'd make mistakes and he'd just have to overlook them."

"Clay, that's not the point."

"Well, what is?

"You really don't know?"

"No."

"The point is, Clay, that all men think alike. They actually think a piece of tail is only for them. That's what it boils down to. You don't give a damn about eating, sleeping or hanging around Cliff, but when you think, for a second, of him laying with me, you go to pieces. Men usually don't like to get married because they get all the tail they want. But when, as in this case, it's close to home, all you think about is your own ill thinking and desire. You forget maybe the woman wants something different. And she's entitled to what she wants, too."

"I guess you're right, Kate, but I still can't see it your way."

"That's because you know I had eyes for you once,

Clay, and what you could've had then – even now had Diamond not come around – just isn't possible anymore. You see now how it goes?"

He relented; she had won. When he thought in terms of Kate and his friend, Diamond, he cringed, but still couldn't believe it fully because he didn't want to."

Clay left the Payday, after buying a drink for Kate, and went to the hotel to sleep. He felt better in a way after he lay figuring out in detail what Kate had said. It made sense all the way. He was about ready to drop off to sleep when he heard the light rap on the door. His instincts told him it was Pet. He opened the door and she slipped in.

"Dad's out at the ranch, so come on while we've got the chance!"

They lay in bed fondling each other. Pet asked questions about the meeting. Clay told her what Kate had said to him, to which Pet said simply, "She loves my brother."

"You approve?"

"I do." After all, who knows who we really are in all this."

She reached down and patted him in excited want and whispered, "Are you going to just lay there with this or are you going to give it to me?"

She got the pleasure she sought, and gave the pleasure that was expected of her not once, but twice.

After a third time, Clay asked, "Don't you ever get enough?"

"Not a bit. I only hope I don't wear it out."

"You won't. And even if you do, there are other ways, you know. And you're crazy about them, don't say that you're not!"

"I know. That's why I don't love the hell out of you too. Sometimes I think you're screwing me to hell and back."

"Is that bad?"

"Not in my book. Most people should do the same."

"I agree, Clay."

"Me, too."

"Then come on, once more."

"Oh, Pet!"

"Oh my foot, come on, and not that way."

"Then how?"

"You know, Clay – kissing."

"You like that, don't you, Pet?"

"When you do it and I do the same to you."

Then and there, between the night and the break of day, their love was proven to be one of the greatest, one that only those in love could begin to understand or even dare to contemplate.

TWENTY-THREE

The first day in July came. At the dairy ranch Diamond and his father were getting ready to come into town to pick up the new bull. They would be bringing the bull back to the ranch.

Pet, still happy from her last affair with Clay, worked in her flower garden. Since her mood was good, she said to her brother, who she now thought the world of, "Cliff, are you going to see your woman?"

He chased her toward the pasture and catching her, tweaked her nose. She screamed and raved.

He said, "I'm going to teach you to keep a civil tongue in your head!"

"You know she's your woman. The whole town knows it. So there!"

He laughed, holding her hand. They walked back to the ranch house porch just like children. Their father stood watching and wiped a tear from his eye, wondering how long this happiness could last in the Phillips family.

"Dad, take this man of Kate's into town, he wants to see his woman."

"Come on, son, we'd better get going if we're going

to get our bull."

Diamond picked up a small stone and tossed it as his sister. She ran into the house, poked her tongue out and him and laughingly said, "There's someone in town waiting for you."

Cliff Diamond Phillips and his father, driving a team and wagon, had a good time laughing all the way to town. The day held brightness not only in their cheer but in the sky as well. Nowhere in Colorado was the endowment of nature so splendid. The rich black earth was virgin soil and the lush green growth atop was evergreen. Pueblo seemed to be bursting at its seems compared to the other towns.

As expected, the 11:30 train brought the Phillips' bull. They had to hold the train up for fifteen minutes while they got the animal off due to the bad spur in the side of the track. Besides Clay, Phillips and Diamond, a few other men were around sizing up the animal.

"It's a good bull, Martin," remarked Clay, as they tied the young black Angus on a short lead rope behind the wagon.

Mr. Phillips, beaming, replied, "I told you he was a fine young animal, Clay."

It didn't take long to return to the ranch where Pet and the workmen all praised the looks of the new Angus. They led him to a pen.

"Well, that's another job done. I'd hate like hell to have this one shot," Mr. Phillips asserted.

"You won't, Pa. And it's funny, no good reason was ever given as to why the other bull was killed."

"I don't know, son. But nobody believed that story Ferrell told about his mistaking it for a black bear."

"Clay never did say if he'd figured out why either,"

remarked Pet.

Cliff lit up a cigarette and said, "I think I'll ride into town tonight and ask him about that."

"Don't tell me you didn't see your girl," teased Pet.

"Pa, you'd better tell that woman there to shut up!"

They all had a good laugh, with Pet enjoying herself the most at her brother's expense.

Later, when all the ranch work was finished up, Diamond washed and shaved. He put on the new spurs that Pet had given him, a clean, ironed shirt and a pair of dark gray trousers. He tied his shoestring tie, letting it hand down, and sat his cream-colored hat at just the right angle. Finally, he strapped on his two cherry-butted colts, got the feel of them, and stepped outside feeling fresh. He saddled his horse and was walking him to the front of the house when Pet saw him.

She called her father and said, "Dad, don't he look handsome?"

The old man threw out his chest and stated with authority, "He should, he comes by it honest. After all, just look at his father!"

She beamed with pride and rushed outside to tell Diamond how he looked.

He thanked her for the compliment and asked, "Wanna ride along into town with me?"

"Not now, Cliff. But you look real nice."

"Thanks, Pet."

Pet watched him cross the fording place with care before returning into the house with an elated feeling of happiness and pride for her brother.

When Diamond got to town, he went to the general store to buy a box of .44 shells. Standing at the counter was Kate. She turned around and saw him, wanting to run into his arms, but holding herself in check.

Jokingly, she said, "Well, Cliff, who's the lucky girl tonight?"

"That's a secret, Kate."

"You wouldn't bet on it, would you?"

Cliff smiled. He made his purchase and, after exchanging a few kind words with the storeowner, he and Kate left the store together.

Kate had a large package, which Diamond carried. The people they passed turned around to stare, after speaking. It seemed as if everyone they met spoke to them by name.

This caused Diamond to ask Kate, "What's happened around this town?"

"Maybe they just see people as people now instead of asses," answered Kate.

"But what stirred them up? Somebody donate something to this town?"

"Well, matter of fact, yes. I did, Cliff."

"What?"

"I'll tell you when we get to the Payday."

They entered the saloon together. Sam nodded and smiled and LeeLee greeted them, "You two make a real nice pair," she said.

Diamond didn't know how to take that remark. He just smiled.

Kate, who was quick on the uptake, said to LeeLee, "Right. So, misses, go fish on the other side of the pond. I'm tired of crab and catfish."

LeeLee laughed loudly. "Kate, I know what you mean."

Cliff laid the package down on Kate's desk and

looked at the woman before him, her green dress perfectly matching the green in her eyes.

Kate said, "You aren't just going to look at me, are you?" The words Kate spoke had magic. The coils of his arms engulfed her. Her lips met his in a new savagery. He squeezed her almost to hurt. She sighed and moaned from the brute strength, with her body pressed closely to his. She felt the hard fullness of him and thought about what LeeLee had said about the steel spring uncoiling. Everything in her cried to receive him. She wanted to feel him inside her. He touched her breasts and gently pressed them. Kate held his hands there and slowly moved her hips against him. She stood on one foot, drawing the other up behind her, and whispered in his ear, "Don't make me spill here, Cliff!"

He squeezed her tighter and pushed his fullness flush against her moving hips. Her words had been in vain. She felt the force of her release thundering down upon her. She pressed tightly against him, and then her limp form sagged.

When Kate opened her eyes, she was sitting in her chair. She held his hand and said, "You hound. I didn't have a chance, did I?"

"You did, and you took it. Don't blame me."

"I knew I wouldn't be able to contain myself if you really kissed me. And I didn't. Now look what you've done to me. I've got to change my clothes."

"Not me, honey. You did it yourself, and in another second, who knows."

"You're still a hound, but next time it won't be dry. Things will be where they belong, then we'll see!"

"Have it your way."

"Don't worry, I will."

Kate kissed him again after she'd come back from changing her clothes. They talked about their state of affairs. Kate began telling him what she'd said on the night of the meeting.

He was disturbed and said, "You shouldn't have, Kate."

"I think so. Now people will begin to understand."

"Let's hope so. At least we saw a little improvement today."

"Cliff, I'm glad you're not bitter. I don't think I could stand that."

"Kate, do you have any idea about who I am?"

"No. Why should I?"

"Well, I'll tell you before too long. Right..."

"Right now, kiss me again and go. I've got work to do."

A few minutes later, Diamond came from the office. He had forgotten to check his guns. He unbuckled them and handed them to Sam and said, "Let's hope I don't need them." Sam made a remark and poured Diamond a glass of his usual.

Diamond was sipping it at the bar, waiting for Kate to get done with her work in the office. Being impatient, he said to Sam, "If the marshal comes in, tell him to come back to the office, please."

Sam agreed to tell him and Diamond took his brandy and milk back to the office with him.

Kate looked like a schoolgirl when he returned to the little room behind the bar. She looked up at him and said, "Run your fingers through it, Cliff, but behave yourself. I don't want to have to change clothes again."

At this moment, Clay walked up to the bar and Sam gave him Diamond's message. He rapped on the office door, opened it and pulled it shut behind him.

Diamond, with his arms still around Kate's waist, asked, "You got my message?"

"That's why I'm here. And, say, don't you two know if you like each other? Or do you still have to keep tasting to find out?" He had a hard cut to his mouth as he spoke.

Cliff laughed and Kate said, "Keep tasting. That way you're sure what's yours."

"What the hell is so funny? You two make me sick with your faces always stuck together."

Cliff didn't care much for Clay's tone of voice, but he tried to make a joke by saying, "Are you jealous?"

"Yeah, of my grandma."

Kate knew Clay had something on his mind and decided to leave the two men alone. As she left she told Diamond, "I'll be back later, sugar!"

Clay winced at her words. Diamond waited until she was out the door. Clay looked at his friend, looking closely and trying to control his rage.

Then Diamond spoke. "I wanted to see you because I've been thinking about that first bull, the bull over at the dairy ranch that was shot. Do you have any idea why it was killed?"

"Yes, and no. Right now it's not clear. Why?"

"I just wanted to know. It doesn't make sense, Clay."

"When I get the right dope on that I'll let you know, Cliff."

"Good. That's what I came to town to find out."

Clay laughed. "You did? Hell, I thought you had another reason for coming into town. Look at you, all spruced up!"

"A man likes to clean up once in a while."

"Look, Cliff, before you go, tell me, did you tell Kate

all that stuff about black people and white people?"

"What stuff do you mean, Clay?"

"White-raisin' Negro women and such."

"I did. And it's the truth! Hell, Clay, I was just explaining the Negro situation against the whites. What's wrong with that?"

"Why didn't you explain it to me?"

"I figured you knew hat much."

"I'm not that smart."

"It's not a matter of being smart; it's a matter of thinking and treating a man the way you yourself would like to be treated."

"Well, it may have truth in it."

"It's not important, as long as we get along all right," Cliff reasoned.

"Hell, I'm trying to do my part," said Clay.

He lit a cigarette and offered Cliff one. Diamond saw Clay was trying to be as fair as he could. His friend was overcoming a lot, just as he himself was. They puffed and blew smoke until Clay smashed his cigarette out and said, "Listen, and please, hear me out. I heard and believed what you told me, I've listened to Kate and I've come to one conclusion."

"And what's that, Clay?"

"You've got to leave this town and take Kate with you if you want her."

"Is this advice or an order?" Diamond asked through clenched teeth.

"Half of both," Clay answered.

Rising from his seat, Diamond demanded, "Better tell me why, Clay. And make it plain."

"When Blair and that gang of his gets back, they'll want four things. First you, then your dad's ranch;

THE ULTIMATE WESTERN NOVEL

they're sure to know about you and Kate so she'll be in the pot too, with me being last on their list.

"You think I could run out on myself and my family and Kate just to avoid a little trouble?"

"That's not the point, Cliff. It will be saving a lot of trouble, especially for you. The rest I can handle."

Diamond didn't like Clay's attitude or his implications. "From what I hear, Clay, Bryant is going all out and now you ask me to play his game and run."

Clay knew this was only partly true, with the rest being he wanted to break Kate and Cliff apart. He just felt it wasn't right. The more he tried to overlook it, the more baffling it became. He resented it.

Diamond took a long time to answer. He thought everything out plain and clear, and saw the whole, true picture. He liked and admired Clay, yet he knew Clay wasn't telling him the full story. He wasn't lying, but wasn't exactly revealing his own personal reasons for wanting Cliff to leave town either.

Diamond spoke, "Clay, now it's time for you to listen, and listen good. You're only telling me some of the truth. Sure, you'd like to see me leave town to keep down trouble and I can see your point. But you aren't really worried about Blair and his gang. Your biggest worry is that Kate and I are doing what you and my sister have already done. How do you think I feel, knowing you're laying Pet out of wedlock? And the hell of it is, I know and trust you to do the right thing. But because Kate is a friend of yours, you hate like hell to think of me going to bed with her. Now that's what you don't like. Because deep down, the rest don't matter a damn, now does it?"

Clay had turned flush. He looked at Cliff and yelled,

"Are you calling me a liar?"

"I am, if you say Kate and I don't worry you the most! Damn the others in town, I just want your friendship most.

"I'll tell you what, Cliff, you are right. I can't stand to think of you laying Kate. What white man could?"

"A lot, when they have any woman they want, even in this town. Do you think Madam LaCall's maid just plays with herself? Remember she's black and so am I. Do you think I should care that she's getting hers from a white man? If she wants a white man, that's her business. She can lay in bed with you or anybody else she pleases as long as she respects me and my right to choose my own love."

The words were hot and sharp when Clay yelled, "I'll make you one last offer, you stubborn bastard. I'm going to make you a deputy, then maybe we'll get somewhere!"

"Well, I refuse that, too. I'll not hide behind the white man's law to kill white men. I know you'll need help when Blair gets back. I'll side with you because I admire you for at least trying to be fair and be my friend."

"Damn you, Cliff, you son of a bitch. You keep making it harder and harder for me. I oughta just knock you flat on your ass."

"That wouldn't be too easy to do. Besides, all you want is a good excuse to hit me, to strike back at me because of Kate. Clay, don't let a piece of tail cause you to lose your head."

"I'm taking more from you, you black bastard, than I've ever taken from any man!"

"And if I know the real man behind that star, Marshal Clinton, you'll take more!"

216

"Shut up, Cliff."

"Shut up yourself, Clay."

"Damn you, Cliff, don't you tell me to shut up."

Before Clay knew it, he had thrown a punch to Diamond's chin, sprawling him against the desk. Clay was sorry, but he sure felt a strong sense of relief.

Diamond could tell he was relieved and said, "All right. You threw it and got half of it off your chest. Now let's go all the way and clear the air completely."

He then threw an exploding right hand, catching Clay on the side of the face.

Both men became a blur of fistic fury. They clasped together as if dancing, but their hands were dealing out breathtaking blows instead of caresses. The force of their struggle against the office door sent both men crashing out into the bar.

Kate screamed and so did the girls. The fighters' shirts were torn and sweaty.

Kate yelled, "Stop them, Sam! Please, stop them! Somebody please stop them, they'll kill each other."

When Sam and a few men came near the two rolling on the floor, both sneered together, "Stay out of this!"

Clay managed to crawl up from the floor first. Diamond jumped up, only to be knocked down again. He bounced up and grabbed Clay and flung him around, landing a few useful blows right to his gut. Clay sprawled over a chair and crashed to the floor. Diamond waited for him to get up. And then he sent him back to the floor with a groan.

Kate yelled, "Cliff! Clay! Please, stop this!"

The two men had no time to answer. Clay slowly crawled from the floor and clinched with Diamond, tearing his shredded shirt completely off him. They fought, throwing all kinds of blows into each other. They clinched again and rolled out the swinging doors onto the sidewalk and into the street.

The whole saloon had emptied into the street, following every move the two men made. No one was cheering. They only had silent admiration for the brute strength matched against brute strength. No one knew what had caused the battle. From Sam, who was standing with Kate and LeeLee, holding the marshal's fallen guns, to everyone else looking on, no one tried to stop it.

Pet and her father were standing on the porch of the hotel when they heard someone yell, "They're fighting like hell – the marshal and Diamond!"

They didn't wait to hear more, but rushed over to the scene and found Kate. They asked her what had happened. She couldn't tell what started it, but relayed the message both men gave her, "Stay out of it!"

Mr. Phillips was heartsick as he watched. Pet, the same as Kate, was anxious for one of them to drop so it would stop. The two women just watched, knowing there was nothing that could be done if that was how the two men wanted it.

Bloody noses, crushed mouths, rumpled hair and bruised bodies. Both men were exhausted and suffering. Their clothes were ripped and both were naked to the waist.

They fell into each other with hammer-like blows. Clay and Diamond had fought from the Payday saloon down to the jail. By the time they had reached the jail, neither could stand up. They crawled on their hands and knees to get to each other. When they met, the strength from their fatigued bodies melted with the dirt, blood and sweat. They laid pitiful slaps on each other before finally collapsing in a heap on the ground.

The moon shone just enough light to make the scene appear gruesome and tranquil.

Someone in the crowd said, "Well, it's all over."

"Who won?" a man asked.

"Who the hell knows," came a reply.

Mr. Phillips looked at his son and his friend and said, "This is a shame. Will some of you men carry both of them into the jail?"

A few of the men took the limp bodies and placed them on cots in the first two cells. They left, leaving only Kate, Pet and Mr. Phillips, who sat shaking his head saying, "It's disgraceful."

"Are you going to leave them here, Dad?"

"It's where they both belong."

Kate, also showing her disgust, remarked, "Come on, Pet, let's go get some things to clean them up with."

The women, with the help of Mr. Phillips, cleaned the two men up to look like human begins again. They didn't bother talking to the men, giving them only cold, damning glances.

Mr. Phillips told them both what he thought of their actions and then walked out into the jail's office. A few minutes later, the women shuffled out.

"Let's go, Pet," said Mr. Phillips.

"I'm staying," she said, "Kate and I have to look after them."

"What, in jail?"

"Why, yes Dad. I'm a big girl now."

"Yes. Yes, of course. That's what I'm worried about."

Kate laughed and poured herself a drink form the bottle she'd brought for the two men. They had been too tired to indulge. "Pet's right," she said, "we'd better stay for a while."

Mr. Phillips stormed off to his hotel muttering, "The two damned fools, fighting like that."

After the town had gotten quiet in the wee hours of the morning, the two women stirred from their naps. Sitting at the marshal's desk, they had talked of many things before they had dozed off. Now they sat, with their skirts hiked up above their knees. Pet looked at her own legs and rubbed them. She patted Kate's legs gently and said, "Kate, I overheard some of the men talking one day and one said that you and I had the prettiest asses in the county."

"That don't surprise me. Men say all sorts of things."

"Well, come on," sighed Pet.

"Come on where?"

"I was just thinking... a good man, after a good fight, needs but one thing, Kate."

"And what's that, Pet?"

"A good woman to give him a damn good piece of loving."

"Pet! The things you say and do!"

"Hell, Kate, I learned it from you. Let's go."

"I'm right with you. There's two damned good men in there."

"I know. And in case they're thinking of fighting again, here are two good pieces of tail that can give them all the fight they want."

"Let's go, Pet. I've got something to get even with Diamond for, and now will be my chance!"

They laughed as they walked back to the cells where the two men were.

TWENTY-FOUR

On the afternoon of the first of July, Blair and his men were in place. In Hank's place, Billy Ferrell rode the train from Denver, with a new man along with Mex. As was planned, when the first coach passed Post Point, all three men swung into action. The new outlaw stepped outside on the crosswalk and climbed up to thc brake on the caboose. Billy Ferrell stepped into the caboose with the Mex behind him.

The guards guarding the money were caught napping with their rifles standing against the car wall. They looked into the ugly mouths of the two .44's pointed at them.

Billy told Mex, "All right, uncouple the car!"

The Mex leaned out of the car and, with his sharp knife, cut the air hose connection and lifted the coupling pin. The train moved faster away, foot by foot. The outlaw on the upper wheel brake turned it with all his strength, hearing the rusty wheels brake and the chain screech. The main cars were already over a mile down the track.

The group with Blair, Texas Red Morgan and the Half-Breed, threw a heavy sapling across the track.

They saw the caboose coming as if it wouldn't stop, but the man on the brake wheel used a brakeman stick as a lever and the caboose began to slow down. When it came upon the tree, the caboose almost jumped the track. They finally managed to stop it about a half a mile further down the track.

Billy and Mex tied up the guard and were lucky the brakeman was somewhere else.

Blair, followed by Texas Red, entered the car and saw the tied guards. His first order was, "Kill them! They know us by now."

Billy's guns spurted flames and the helpless men rolled over in death.

"Now, let's see," said Blair.

They waited until the lid was lifted and saw the currency and two boxes of minted gold pieces. Blair helped them carry the heavy boxes out saying, "This is it, boys, the jackpot!"

With great speed they broke open the strong boxes and stuffed their saddlebags full. Two hundred and fifty thousand dollars in gold and paper money made the saddlebags bulge. Had there been more, they would have had to stuff their shirts.

Blair ordered, "Well, men, set fire to that caboose and let's ride!"

They found a coal lantern and sprinkled oil all over the car and lit it. When it caught real good, Blair yelled, "Let's go for leather!"

The six men rode hard and fast to their next stop, where fresh horses were waiting. They changed everything and threw the heavy, money-filled saddlebags on fresh horses.

"All right, Breed," said Blair, "you and Spike burn

the shack and the saddles. Shoot them horses. We don't need them anymore."

Again they rode, making better time with fresh horses under them. At their next stop, some fifteen minutes later, they went through the same routine. One of the gang had fresh horses waiting. Blair issued the same instructions and his men carried them out while he rode on to Pueblo. The shack and the horses were disposed of, leaving no clear trail for anyone to follow.

On the last leg to Pueblo, only Blair, Texas Red and Billy were left to bring the money into town. They had done this so often it was like clockwork.

They came in along the river, riding for about a mile or two; then cut across the grassy slope which brought them out near the livery stable.

The town was asleep. No lights could be seen anywhere, with the exception of the moon. They slowed and walked their horses down the main street to the bank. Billy held the horses while Texas Red and Blair carried the five heavy bags into the bank.

The banker was there waiting. His beady little eyes flashed at the sight of the bulging bags. "Right into the safe with it," he said.

"All right, Bryant," said Blair, "you get it ready. The boys will be in later."

The banker, closing the door behind them, said, "I'll see you later, Blair."

As quietly as they had come, they went. The plan of a few months waiting had paid off. And paid in a handsome sum!

TWENTY-FIVE

For two days no one saw the marshal. He stayed in his hotel room recovering from the stiffness and aches that resulted from his fight with Diamond. He laughed to himself. The fight had done three things. It made him appreciate Diamond more; it relieved him of the pent up anger and it confirmed the fact that Diamond was indeed a friend he could count on. He figured he needed the fight to make him realize that the color of a man made no difference to intelligent people. Misfortune and ignorance had to be taught.

He admired Kate for helping him understand something about the Negro people that he never knew, and felt grateful to Diamond for standing up against him and making him realize the basic birth rights of every man. Either way, it made no man more than any other except how much forgiveness a man had in his heart toward his fellow being.

Clay washed and dressed; looking at the soiled clothes he had worn. He put cigarettes in his pockets, buckled on his guns, after cleaning and examining them, and noticed it was near time for lunch.

When he came downstairs he spoke to the waitress. She took his order. The way she looked at his crotch made him uneasy. Her mind was easily read. She brought out his lunch and was just about to sit down at his table when three other men came into the room to eat. Seeing the other men, she looked at them and cursed. "Damn, I was hoping to get you again."

Clay smiled in relief. The morning air, clinging to the shadows of the building, was a refreshing boon on his hot face. He rubbed his chin and thought, "Jesus, that man hits like a kicking horse."

The marshal felt good, sort of like having a physical and spiritual readjustment. Lighting a cigarette, he started on his rounds. His first stop was the station, where the station agent handed him two wires.

The first one he read was from his Uncle Mart, saying that the last money he had inquired about was indeed stolen. This was the money the banker had given Mr. Phillips when he cashed Kate's check. Clay was glad to hear this.

The second wire was from the sheriff in Denver, telling him about their recent robbery and how much money was stolen. The wire went on to say that two guards were killed and that the robbery had taken place at Post Point.

He folded both messages, pocketed them, and then began walking with haste. He had never been out in the vicinity of Post Point before. He hurried back to the jail and got Old John to tell him how to get there. The old swamper gave Clay the information freely, who, in turn, left orders not to tell anyone where he was headed. The old man just nodded his head.

Baldy was a bit frisky, but after a few miles of giving him his head on the open range, he settled down to an easy walk. Clay had no intention of following a trail. He just wanted to check over the scene of the crime. He knew that the robbery had taken place three days ago; the wire had said the first of July.

***

Blair took advantage of the two days without the marshal out and about town. He first went to see Clark Bryant at the bank and was amused to learn that Clay and Diamond had gotten into one hell of a brawl. He smiled at the thought of a fight coming between the two. He knew that he could handle each one separately.

Blair was not, however, amused when the banker told him about Kate spoiling the citizens meeting. Blair raged, "That bitch will pay for that!"

After explaining to Bryant that the men would be in, as usual, to collect their shares, the latest job netting each man a neat twelve and a half thousand dollars, the rest going to himself and the banker, of course, Blair raced from the bank to find Texas Red Morgan. They whispered and laughed at the turn of events. Blair told Red they'd wait until the boys came into town, then strike. Red agreed. He cursed in telling Blair about Hank's brother Ripper being killed by Diamond.

Blair replied, "I heard that, too, but we'll fix the whole bunch when the boys come in."

***

Out at the dairy ranch things were running smoothly. Diamond, like Clay, was sore and stiff, but a few days after the fight he'd gone back to doing his share of the work and taking, in stride, all the kidding from the other men and Pet. He only got distaste from his father. But all in all, he wasn't sorry about the fight. He knew that Clay would feel better, but wondered what their relationship would be like now. He had forgiven Clay but got depressed whenever he thought about how Clay would feel toward him now. Pet had teased him about being a tiger, to which he'd dropped his head in a bit of shame. He decided not to go near town for at least a week.

Meanwhile, Clay had found Post Point and the scene of the robbery; a lonely place surrounded by dry sagebrush and cactus. His sharp eyes had searched the area but found nothing. In the wilderness the wind and shifting sands continuously kept things moving.

He saw where the caboose had been burned. Many horse tracks were still visible on the tracks' hard surface. He looked at these, trying to pick out a clear marking.

On his way back to town, he trailed the group tracks that had left sort of a rut in the sand, and came to a place where more tracks converged. Since this was harder soil, the tracks were clearer. He studied this new meaning for a bit and looked at the footprints. His diagnosis was right: the boot prints showed that men had changed horses here. He looked to see where the other horses had come from and saw a plain trail going off to his left. He trailed those tracks for about three miles, seeing nothing but a lone jackrabbit sitting on his hind legs and staring right back at him.

Then he saw the burned out shack. Clay slid from the saddle and looked around. The scene made him physically ill. A sickening aroma hung in the dead horse's forehead. The bits of charred wood, saddles and blankets made it clear that the gang had changed to fresh mounts, slaughtered their tired horses and set fire to the shack.

The marshal returned to the open prairie, where

the tracks converged. He trailed the new set of tracks a great distance before finding the second burned out shack with the smell of dead horse flesh in the air. He knew Blair and his men were cruel, but now he realized just how ruthless and heartless these men were.

He followed this trail for the remainder of the day, returning to the sleeping town of Pueblo long after midnight.

In bed at the hotel, he made up his mind as to who all was in this gang, but had no actual proof of anything. He decided to wait and see how Blair would act when he saw him. From this, he'd form a plan. Everything fitted into a pattern. He knew the key was Blair, but proving it was the big job; the job he had been hired on to do.

During the rest of the week Clay stayed out of the Payday. He had, from different points, been watching men come and go, entering and leaving the bank – staying only a few minutes before they'd leave. Clay figured this happened at least six or maybe seven times. When he saw Billy Ferrell enter and leave the bank as the others had done, he knew them all to be part of Blair's gang. He kept a close eye on Blair and Texas Red Morgan, seeing them talk with the other men he'd seen. His mind was made up to get to the bottom of this business once and for all.

At the gambling table in the Payday, money was flowing heavily. Clay walked over to watch a few hands. Sitting in on the game were Blair, Texas Red and the Mex.

Blair made the first remark. "Understand you had a little trouble, Marshal."

"You understand wrong, Blair."

"I'd never let a black bastard whip me!" stated Texas Red.

Clay ignored the remark and kept his eyes on the crisp new paper money in the game. He had every idea that this was the stolen money from the train robbery and realized that Blair and his men used the money right out in the open because they feared no trouble from the law, or from anyone else for that matter.

Clay asked, "You print your own money, Blair?"

"You might say I use it new because I don't like my hands to get dirty," Blair smirked.

"Good idea."

"It's nothing, Marshal. All the banks carry good money. All you've got to do is go in and ask for it."

"Yeah," Clay said, "I never thought of that, Blair."

Clay walked over to the bar where Kate greeted him. "Long time no see, stranger. You tired of our company?"

"No, on the contrary, I think I've really come to appreciate it."

Kate understood why he'd said that and remarked, "I haven't seen your friend, and mine, since the battle royal."

"Don't worry, Kate, he'll be around."

"Clay, I don't think you'll tell me, but I have to ask. What was all that about?"

"I'll tell you this much Kate, it's because of that fight that I can see you as a woman with the right to have who the hell you want. But other than that, it's a thing your kind of women don't think about."

But Clay was wrong, Kate understood. She said, "What you're saying, Clay, is that you don't think I'll marry Diamond."

Clay didn't answer.

She asked, "Don't you care if I marry the fellow?"

"Not a bit. And you can give him anything you want to."

"You mean some more, don't you?"

"I... er... I'll see ya later, Kate. I got a man to see."

"Right," she said.

She felt good watching him leave. It brought her closer to him knowing his heart and mind were clear.

***

Later in the afternoon, Clay rode out to the dairy ranch. The first person he saw was Pet. She kissed him and teased him by saying, "I thought you were afraid to come out here."

"I am afraid. I can't get enough of you!"

"Good. Now let's see you prove it."

He looked around and, seeing no one in sight, pressed her gently between his thighs saying, "Don't know what to do with a woman like you."

She reached down and felt him growing hard under her touch. "I do," she said. "Give it to me and keep me happy with what I need and want."

She looked at him questionably and shrugged her shoulders, then called her brother from the house.

The two men faced each other for the first time since the night of the fight.

Diamond asked, "You want me?"

"Yeah, I do. But there's a woman in town who wants to see you even more, and if you don't take care of that little business I'll have to kick your ass good. That last scrap won't be nothing compared to the next one."

For the first time Diamond laughed. He asked, "Is that an order, Clay?"

"You're damn right it is."

Diamond walked form the porch, knowing everything between them was all right. He looked around for Pet, but she had slipped away.

"You know, Clay, that left fist of yours could kill a man."

"That right of yours ain't bad by a long shot, Cliff."

Diamond wanted to ask more questions but didn't think the time was right.

Clay mounted his horse, leaned from his saddle and said, "Damn you, if you don't marry Kate, I'll shoot you on sight."

Diamond knew this was his friend's honest feeling. Inside he was a well of happiness and Clay could see it.

"Before I go, I want to tell you that Blair is back with all his men. I suspect they're going to strike out soon, but I can't say when so I'm ordering you – when you're in town, don't take your guns off."

Diamond knew what he meant and agreed. Then he said, "Send me word. I've got a stake in this when it starts."

"I won't promise you that, this is my job. But I do kind of like having you around to guard my back."

"And you mine, old friend. Wait, before you go…" Diamond called his sister and when she came he said, with a grin, "Better taste your woman, Clay, before you leave."

He ducked her swinging fist as she laughed and shouted, "I'll do that. I'll get even, you hound."

TWENTY-SIX

Blair's men all converged in his office as their plans were being made. Blair had assigned the new man, Tully, to watch the saloon as a precautionary measure. They had even brought Hank into town with his half-healed shoulders. Blair had him hidden away in the attic of Madam LaCall's shop. He was given a double-barreled shotgun. Hank's orders were to shoot the second he saw Clay and Diamond together. Blair had said, "Blow both of them to hell!"

Billy Ferrell was given the job of ambushing either man if they came his way, as was the Half-Breed. The Mex was to work his own way, with Texas Red Morgan and Blair together, patrolling the street.

These were the six men Blair trusted most. The others weren't to have a hand in the fun but, instead, were to stay out at the ranch and look after things.

It was the morning of a new day; a day that held the promise of being hot and uncomfortable, when Clay emerged to make his regular rounds. He started with Madam LaCall's, which turned out to be a lucky break for the marshal.

"Marshal," Madam LaCall confided, "sometimes I

think I'm losing my mind."

"Now what makes you say that, Madam?"

"I keep hearing sounds up in the attic, and I even think I smell cigar smoke sometimes."

Clay looked pensively up at the attic. "You want I should take a look?"

"No, Marshal, I suppose it's all right. Just the imagination of an old woman, I guess." Clay left the Madam's shop and crossed the street. He raised his head high as if looking at the sky and turned his eyes on the attic window. His sharp sight detected the white swirl of smoke as he saw a figure dart from the corner of the window. He was convinced that the Madam wasn't out of her mind at all. There was someone up there.

He looked down the street and saw the man called Tully standing in front of the Payday. He began to get a sick feeling in his stomach and knew a trap had been spread out around him.

Blair and Texas Red emerged from a store, saw the marshal and headed his way. Seeing Texas Red loosen his gun, Clay knew trouble was coming.

When they drew near, Blair quickly glanced up at Madam LaCall's attic window, giving away his knowledge of a man stashed there.

"Morning, Marshal," said Blair, "hope you have a nice day."

"Oh, I will," said Clay. "You'd just better hope your plan works, Blair."

The two men hurried off, leaving the marshal where he stood on the street. Clay knew it must be Hank in the attic window watching him, but he couldn't figure where the rest of Blair's men were. He retraced his steps and entered Madam LaCall's shop. He told her in a whisper to go over to the hotel and stay there. The Madam and her maid, Emma, did as Clay had instructed.

Clay peeped from the front window just in time to see a man leap across the roof of the bank. He cursed himself for staying in the shop so long. He sighed with relief as he saw Kate walking up the street. As she passed the window, he beckoned to her and she entered.

"What's..."

"Shh." He pointed upstairs and whispered, "Listen, you stay off the street. Hell is about to be released here."

He wasn't sure what Kate would do, but he let her go. He knew he was trapped by entering the Madam's shop the second time, and now he wished he'd asked Kate to go and fetch Diamond.

Kate managed to get near the end of the street. She took the reins of a horse and climbed into the saddle. She didn't know whose horse it was, nor did she care. As she mounted her dress flew up past her knees and the men who saw her all got a good look. Kate didn't particularly care - she was on a mission. She was riding to get a friend who was needed desperately.

Because of Clay's visit to the ranch yesterday, Diamond had decided to ride into town. He had left that morning; right after the ranch work was done. Both Pet and Diamond were jogging along when they saw the woman rider headed straight for them.

"Cliff, that's Kate!" exclaimed Pet.

Like a shot, Diamond surged forward with Pet right on his heels. Kate was almost breathless when they reached her.

Kate gasped, "Trap! They've got him pinned down in Madam LaCall's shop."

She didn't need to say anything more. Diamond was off, his big blue roan beginning to lather from the heat of the fast pace. He left Kate and Pet behind to decide for themselves whether to follow him into town or return to the ranch. He was hoping they would return to the ranch, but knew they wouldn't.

Diamond took a chance winding his horse, but it got him into town in a hurry. He tied the animal at the end of the street behind the harness shop. He hadn't heard any shots. He knew that might be a bad sign. He raced down the alley, looking and listening with a sense of alertness that keeps a man alive in gunplay. He was in back of his father's hotel when a knife whizzed by his head and thudded into the siding. He threw himself on the ground and crawled between the hotel and Madam LaCall's place.

Clay, who was still in the shop, had his guns drawn, but nothing to start on. He saw the door being pushed open by a foot. He froze and trained his guns.

A voice, in a low whisper, called, "Clay, you in here?"

"Come on in and join the party. I'd rather see you right now than a million dollars. How did you find me?"

"Kate told me."

Diamond slid inside, smiling. Clay pointed up at the attic and told Diamond who was there. Cliff nodded. Clay then threw two quick shots into the ceiling. The man moved. The flush had worked.

Cliff followed the sound of the move with four more shots. They heard a groan, then a crash.

To make sure, Clay put two more shots directly into the sound of the fall, and reloaded. From one of the eight bullet holes came a dropping of blood. The men only nodded to each other.

They found their way to the attic through a trap door, going up with their guns ready. There would be no more trouble from Hank. His riddled form lay still in death.

"Bring his shot gun with you," Diamond said as they both returned downstairs. He looked at Clay. "That's a nasty little toy he had, isn't it?"

"We can't stay here. Let's go out and do some over-due housecleaning," Clay said.

"I'm with you, Marshal. Shall we go?"

Diamond emerged from the shop, with Clay covering him. A shadow from the top of the bank rose up to be met by two shots that tore his face apart. Cliff raised his hand to Clay in a gesture of thanks.

Clay joined Cliff and they scooted across the street. They saw a head appear, then duck back.

"Clay, I'm crossing over to the other side. I'll cover you and you cover me." It was called cross covering, something few men could trust.

They walked slowly to the Payday. Texas Red came out of the saloon, his quick eyes catching Diamond first but then Clay caught his attention by shouting, "I want you, Red, as a special gift!"

The men laughed with confidence as they stepped out into the street.

Clay put his guns back into their holsters and yelled, "Whenever you're ready, Red. I want to make sure you peep and watch the devil's sister undress when you go to hell."

There was a flash and a blur. Only Diamond saw Texas Red's action at the sound of the exchanged shots.

Cliff saw Texas Red look away. Texas Red Morgan had sprung to his feet again, only to be met by a hail of lead from Clay's guns a second time. He stayed down this time, his guts spilling like water.

Again they marched down their side of the street. Cliff caught a flash of sunlight and yelled, "Duck, Clay!"

As he yelled, his bullets came within inches of Clay's back and found their resting place in the chest of the Half-Breed. He fell across Clay, his blade shining in the sun.

Clay rolled towards where the Half-Breed had been standing between the buildings to avoid the reflex thrust of the knife.

The new man, Tully, had tried to take advantage of Clay falling when Diamond yelled, but Clay rolled over and was shooting as he fell. Tully looked surprised, walked into the street and crumpled up in a heap, with the middle of his head looking like two red, gaping eyes.

Clay was aware that the sound of all the gunshots would cause people to peer out the windows. He just hoped no one would come out into the street. He waved for Diamond to come over. They talked for a minute or so and then Clay disappeared, running down the street near the jail. The ruse worked. Billy Ferrell ducked out of the Payday, followed closely by Blair.

Diamond ordered, "Hold it, Blair! Don't you move. The marshal wants you."

Billy stopped short when Clay stepped directly in front of him, facing him at arms-length. Billy didn't try for his gun. Instead, he swung. Clay ducked and brought an uppercut to the man's chin. Billy fell backwards and, in doing so, he clawed for his gun. He was spun around by a slug, and he staggered and sank as if kneeling to his death.

Clay came over to where Blair was standing, covered by Cliff's guns. "Let's go to your office. I want to hear and see something, Blair."

With the self-styled town boss between them, they escorted Blair to his office. Blair smiled to himself, just waiting for the right moment to act. He figured neither Clay nor Diamond knew about his hideout gun.

Diamond stepped from the sidewalk first. Blair hesitated just a step, causing Clay to step from the sidewalk a step behind Diamond, giving Blair the advantage of being a step behind both men. Blair, in that flash of a moment, snapped his elbow and the deadly hidden gun leapt into his hand. He pressed the small two-shot Derringer into Clay's back.

"That's far enough, Marshal."

Clay halted. Diamond turned, but it was too late. But Blair had gotten the full drop on Clay.

"Stay where you are, darkie, or I'll blow hell out of your friend."

Diamond was about two feet from Clay, his guns out and ready. Blair was standing directly behind Clay. He moved Clay back with him, back into the street as he eased away from Diamond. He was planning to hold Clay hostage, and so far he was doing well.

People had begun to gather outside, watching and wondering at the turn of events. Even Kate and Pet were standing in front of the Payday, their hearts in their mouths.

It was Kate who said, "Lord! Blair's got Clay and Cliff is helpless."

All the onlookers were watching the drama of gunmanship never to be forgotten in Colorado history.

Diamond had moved into the street. Blair had moved about fifteen feet away and this was exactly what Diamond had wanted.

He waited, becoming a bundle of hard, cold steel.

Blair yelled, "Don't come any closer, black boy!" Then, pressing the gun hard into Clay's back he sneered, "And don't you try ducking either, you bastard."

When Blair was near the saloon, he yelled to Diamond again. "You can put your pop gun away now, darkie."

Cliff's heart sank. This was just the split second and precise thing he wanted. He had the distance he needed.

Everyone heard Blair yell again, "Put 'em away, I said!"

"Here goes, Clay," Diamond said to himself.

He brought his guns up and spun them around and into the holsters. His keen, almost giant, eyes saw Blair was watching his every move. Spinning his guns into their holsters would cause the man a second of doubt and fixation.

Just as quickly as his guns were holstered, the people saw Diamond rear back. His knees buckled slightly. He had his balance. With the same motion he used to spin the guns into the holsters, he withdrew them even more quickly. No one saw the guns come out; they only thought they saw them go in. The first two slugs whizzed by Clay's head, less than an inch away. Clay was a statue of ice. He figured Cliff for just this type of shooting.

Blair's reflexes made him duck slightly to his right side to meet the second two delayed shots within a split second of the first two.

The force of the bullets had vanished in his forehead. Clay turned around and looked at the fallen man, feeling just a tad bit sorry for him. "What a fool," Clay thought. It was sickening to look at Blair's figure lying there.

***

The argument in Pueblo began that night. Had Diamond fired two shots or four shots? People swore he never holstered his guns and some folks even called each other liars, arguing that no man could shoot like that!

TWENTY-SEVEN

Diamond stood with Clay. People crowded around. Pet looked sad and so did Kate.

Diamond turned to walk away and faced his father. "I heard you were good, son."

"Not anymore, Pa. I'm giving my guns to Pet for her children."

The people around them thought they heard what Cliff had called Mr. Phillips, but didn't believe their ears until a man stepped from the crowed and asked, "Mr. Phillips, can I have my job back? I'm real sorry about how I acted."

Mr. Phillips, with a proud expansion of his chest, said, loud enough for all to hear, "Don't ask me, I'm not running the ranch anymore. Ask my son, Cliff."

Diamond answered without being asked, "As far as I'm concerned, Sandy, you've never been off the payroll."

The crowed cheered at this statement.

Cliff Diamond Phillips found Kate looking at him with awe, mixed with what some women call admiration.

"So that's who you are."

"I'm afraid so, Kate."

He unbuckled his guns and said, "I promised these to my sister for her children."

She rose up on tiptoe, whispering in his ear, "I'm glad you're putting them away, but why can't you save them for your own child?"

"Me?"

"Yes, you," said Kate. "If it's not yours, you're taking the blame anyway."

He frowned in astonishment at hearing Kate's revelation.

***

The whole town was joyous after the burials of Blair and his men. Kate opened the bar until six o'clock that evening with free drinks. So did her competition, the Dipper Saloon.

Clay and Diamond, along with Mr. Phillips and Mr. Graystone, had work to do. They went over to the bank, got the banker and brought him over to Blair's office. They broke open the door to the roll-top desk and went through the papers and files. The only thing of interest they found was a telegram from Denver addressed to Mr. Clark Bryant, stating the shipment would leave the mint on the first of July. It read, "Will wait your reply. Signed, Elmer Bryant."

"So, your brother was the inside man. Do you want to tell me the rest of it?"

"No," Bryant shouted. "I'll not divulge bank business."

When they found nothing else in Blair's office, they headed back to the bank. When the banker refused to open the safe, Clay got a clerk to open it. Inside they found a land grant issued to a Julius Lee Heris; one daughter, Sarah Lee.

Handing the old land grant to Mr. Phillips, Clay said, "Know anything about this?"

"I should say so, I do. This is Cliff's mother. Her father was who the government gave the land grant to."

"Now you know why Blair killed the bull and wanted the dairy ranch."

"I do, indeed. But how did he get a hold of this land grant? Do you know, Bryant?"

Bryant made no reply.

Clay looked at the money inside plus all they had taken from the gang. All three men agreed it was the stolen money.

The banker finally confessed that he had stolen the land grant from the office of the U.S. Land Commission in Texas, where he had met Blair, who was a lawyer. Working together, they had come to Pueblo to set up the bank.

It was as Clay had suspected. Nobody would suspect the bank as being a vault for the loot, and it was a good way to circulate the money.

The banker confessed everything about the gang and how they'd operated, and, to Clay's satisfaction, even told how they'd traveled on the last job. He said the money was to be used to buy Blair the governorship.

They stayed until all the gang's business was straightened out, so Clay could report to his uncle.

The bank was closed until agents could come from Austin to check on the accounts, frauds and other matters. The banker was put in jail.

Clay and Cliff had dinner with Kate and Pet in the hotel that night. The hero was given more to drink than he could stand. Kate and Pet each took her man and put him to bed.

The town was wild with celebration.

The next afternoon, Clay sent his report to his uncle and asked him to come to Pueblo, bringing bank people to straighten out the financial affairs of the town. He asked him to wire all parties concerned, and also asked him to bring more cigarettes.

Diamond had been in the Payday all afternoon. The jail was kept by Old John, who was cursing the banker for being an old fool. The banker had been brooding at having lost it all, blaming Phillips and his black son. He waited until Old John opened the cell door to bring his lunch to make his move. He pushed right over the older man and ran out into the office. Grabbing the sawed-off shotgun, he darted into the street in a rage. He saw Mr. Phillips going up on the hotel porch. He fired both barrels.

Mr. Phillips grabbed his side and fell.

Someone yelled, "Bryant just killed Martin Phillips!"

The news spread to the Payday. Diamond rushed into Kate's office, buckled on the cherry-butted .44's and ran to where people were carrying his father into the hotel. His eyes were filled with tears.

He walked away saying, "I'll be back, Pa."

Clay came up the street from the station. Someone had gone to get him and told him about the shooting. He heard four shots in the alley behind the hotel. When he got there, he found the banker sprawled on the ground, never to move again. He knew it was Diamond's work. A large lump came up in his throat, and he cried for the first time.

He walked out of the alley and saw Diamond standing up the street. He called out to him, "Cliff, witnesses saw Bryant shoot your father, but Bryant was a federal prisoner. I'll have to ask you to come down to the jail until the folks from Austin arrive."

"Clay, I told you, I won't ever be taken to jail."

"Cliff, use your head. I'm behind you, I'm your friend."

"I know that, Clay, but I can't afford to chance it with the men from Austin. They don't know me like you do."

The street was lined with people. Someone sent for Pet and Kate who were in the hotel with Mr. Phillips.

Clay pleaded again, "Cliff, I have to take you to jail. Don't make my job any harder."

"I'm sorry, Clay. I was there once and I won't stand for going back."

Clay understood the statement that a Negro suffered in jail at the mercy of a white man, yet he also knew that Diamond wouldn't be taken alive. As Marshal, he couldn't let Diamond go, the law damned him.

"Cliff, this is the last time. I'm coming to take you in."

"You won't."

They walked towards each other in slow, measured steps until Diamond said, "That's far enough, Clay. Don't take another step!"

People were standing with mouths agape and hearts in their throats. They were watching two experts about to draw their guns.

Clay looked straight at Diamond and took two more steps.

Diamond demanded, "When you take the next step, Clay, draw."

Clay was calm and dedicated to his job. He had to

bring Cliff in or forever be damned as a quitter and a yellow marshal. He wasn't going to be either, and he knew Cliff was thinking about that, too. He made one more step.

Diamond had his eyes glued on Clay's feet. He didn't watch his hands because he knew Clay couldn't outdraw him. When Clay made the last step, Diamond drew with a quicker streak than before. His guns cleared leather. Folks saw them deliberately pointed at the sky for a split second. Then they heard the two shots and saw the man's hands drop to his sides. They saw him spin around and stride off.

Clay watched as Diamond made his play. He saw the black man's hands dart down towards his sides, making Clay think in terms of beating his man to the draw. With steel eyes glued on the face of his friend, now his foe, Clay's hands sped like lightning to his guns. As he moved with deft quickness, his guns were drawn, hammers cocked and fingers pulling the triggers.

It was too late to recall his shot, for in that moment of stark seriousness his eyes told the full story of regret. He watched as his bullets struck Diamond in the back. He had no way of knowing how Diamond would react except to draw his guns.

The crowd could have been made of stone, for not a whisper passed through the stillness after the sound of Clay's guns. They could see with their eyes and feel in their hearts the regret Clay was feeling at this moment.

The marshal, in a deep state of pride and disgust, walked to where his fallen friend lay, looked down in disbelief and realized in a flash what had really happened. He tore the badge from his chest, unbuckled